Lightning at the Hanging Tree

The rider went by the name of Mike Clancey as this was the name inside his watch, but many people during his travels called him Lightning.

He was too late to stop a hanging and the men were far away by the time he reached the lonely swinging figure of a middle-aged man. When a youth arrived on the scene Lightning found out that the hanged man was his father. Why had he been hanged, and why did this youth seem strange?

Soon the two were to ride together in a pitiless search for the killers.

By the same author

Reluctant Outlaw
The Yellow Bandanna
Lightning Hits Glory Town
The Outlaw's Woman
Outlaws' Loot
Kinsella's Revenge
Smoky Hill Trail
They Called Him Lightning

Lightning at the Hanging Tree

Mark Falcon

A Black Horse Western

ROBERT HALE · LONDON

© Mark Falcon 2008
First published in Great Britain 2008

ISBN 978-0-7090-8553-9

Robert Hale Limited
Clerkenwell House
Clerkenwell Green
London EC1R 0HT

www.halebooks.com

Typeset by
Derek Doyle & Associates, Shaw Heath
Printed and bound in Great Britain by
Antony Rowe Limited, Wiltshire

For Keith Pickering and his friends in some of Bedford's Heavy Metal Bands who asked that their names appear in this book.

CHAPTER ONE

The rider eased his mount to a stop beside a creek and dismounted.

'This seems like a good spot for the night, boy,' he said to his horse. A wry smile crossed his lips just then as he realized that he was talking to his horse more often of late, not that Thunder minded. In fact it seemed to tighten the bond between them. The man spent far more time with his horse than in human company, and lately he became aware that he was lonely.

He knew he needed a shave and a change of clothes. There was not much left of the shirt he was wearing. The material of the sleeves and front were burnt by fire a couple of weeks before as he searched for a young girl inside her burning house. As fate would have it, she had been abducted and kept prisoner by the man who, it turned out, was her real father. With his help he had made sure she received her inheritance.

As he started to prepare a meal before turning in for the night he began to think over the times he could easily have settled down with one of the women he had come across on his search for his identity. It would have been so easy, but he knew he had to ride on and find out who the dark-haired girl was in the small picture inside his pocket watch. His wife? His mother? And what was *his* name? The one inscribed inside the watch: MIKE CLANCEY?

A doctor had said that his memory might return one day, but could not give a definite time. Meanwhile the man who gave his name as Mike Clancey would travel in search of a town called Lodestone which was also inscribed on the watch. He called himself Mike Clancey – but others called him Lightning – justifiably so.

Fifty miles away, to the north east, a gang of men were also bivouacking for the night. There were five of them: Fionbhar Carter, known as Finny; the Young brothers, Matt and Danny; Adam Billington and Nick Bryant. They had ridden together for just over a year and had met whilst in prison.

'We need another bank to rob, Finny,' said Billington as he arranged his blanket roll on a sandy patch of ground near a creek.

'It needs to be a bigger one than the last,' Bryant added. 'It was hardly worth the trouble.'

Finny, the eldest by a couple of years, nodded. 'It beats getting a regular job though, don't it?' He grinned.

'More exciting, I'll admit,' Danny Young added.

'Who'd employ any of us anyhow? None of us is good at anything much, 'cept using a gun,' Matt Young pointed out.

The men, all in their twenties, had by now arranged their bedding for the night. They were running short of supplies and the evening meal was frugal.

'Play us a tune, Finny,' Matt asked his friend. 'Mebbe it'll make us forget how hungry we are.'

Finny grunted. 'I doubt it, but I'll give it a go.'

Carter took his guitar from the pommel of his saddle and started playing something he had made up himself – a rousing ballad of derring-do.

The cockerel always crowed at sun-up and was Matty Hayes's wake up call. Her father was still snoring loudly behind the curtained-off part of the room. It would be another hour or so before he finally woke up.

After dressing and washing her face from a bowl of water from the bucket near the stove she fed the chickens and collected the eggs. She now had three dozen to take into town that morning. But not before picking a basket of peaches and apples from the orchard outside the small cabin. It was no use asking her father to help her. In fact he had been no use to her at all since her mother died nine years ago. She had realized some time before that Joe Hayes was using the death of his wife as the reason for his continual drunken state. When he was not drinking he was gambling away what little money Matty earned from the eggs and fruit. She did not know how much longer she could carry on. It was a life of drudgery for her and it seemed as if it would never end.

Joe Hayes eventually surfaced and ate the bowl of gruel Matty put before him.

'What's this muck? I need something better than this, girl!' he growled.

'And I deserve better than this treatment from you, Pa!' she flung back at him. 'Things have gotta change around here – or I'm leaving!' Matty threatened.

'Huh!' Joe scoffed. 'And where the hell do you think you'll go?'

Matty hesitated for a moment. 'I don't know, but anywhere would be better than here. If I didn't work my fingers to the bone you'd have starved to death by now.'

Joe Hayes growled. He knew she was right, but he refused to admit it to her.

'I'm going into town this morning,' Matty said.

'So am I,' Joe replied.

'I've got to pay off what we owe at the store before they'll let us have any more groceries.'

Joe got up from his chair and Matty saw the expression on his face change.

'I'll take the money into them. Where is it – in the pot?' he asked, walking towards the big china pot on the dresser.

Matty became alarmed at this.

'No need, Pa. I've got to take the eggs and fruit into the store, so I'll pay them.'

Joe took out the few dollar bills, put them into the pocket of his trousers and gave her a smile.

'I'll save you the trouble, Matty. I'll be off now.'

Matty's heart fell. She knew the money would not enter the general store. But it would definitely appear in the saloon. Apart from hitting her father over the head or shooting him, she knew she was unable to stop him.

Matty arrived in Salado at around noon. The basket of eggs had travelled safely as she had found a way of hanging the basket over a pole so that it swung rather than bounced on the bottom of the wagon. She jumped down and wound the horse's reins over the hitching rail outside the store.

'Good morning, Matty,' Mrs Webb said as Matty carried the eggs up to the counter.

'Good morning, Mrs Webb. I've got some fruit outside.'

'Linus, help Matty bring it in!'

Linus Webb hurried after her and they carried in four baskets between them.

Mrs Webb added up how much she should give Matty for the load.

'That's six dollars, Matty – less of course the three dollars you owe us from last time.'

Matty's mouth dropped open. 'But Pa said he'd call in this morning and pay you, Mrs Webb.'

The woman shook her head. 'Sorry, Matty. He hasn't come by yet. Maybe he's called in somewhere else first?'

Matty nodded. She knew Mrs Webb was well aware of her father's habit.

'Can I have a side of bacon, Mrs Webb?'

This left Matty with one dollar for herself.

Matty got back on the wagon and started back for home. She reached the saloon just as her father came tumbling out through the batwing doors.

At the same time five men rode up and dismounted. They all looked as if they had been living rough for some time and all grew their hair long. The first stepped up to the boardwalk and came level with Matty. She noticed the look in his eye as they regarded each other.

Fionbhar Carter held out his hand to Matty. 'May I help you down, miss?' he asked courteously.

She ignored him and called to her father.

'Pa, come on home!'

Fionbhar looked down at the man at his feet.

'He's your pa?' he asked, looking up at Matty.

She gave a slight nod in reply.

'How could a little runt like you, have such a beautiful daughter?' he asked as he pulled Joe to his feet.

Finny shook his head in amazement. The other four of the gang with him were sniggering.

'You must have a beautiful mother, that's all I can say, miss,' Finny said.

'She was,' Matty replied. 'Pa, get on your horse and come home, now!'

Finny still had Joe by one arm.

'I'll take care of him, miss. You go home. Are there any more there like you?'

'No,' Matty replied curtly. She watched as her father was escorted back into the saloon. What would happen to him after that, Matty was not sure whether she cared. But deep down she knew she always would. She flicked the reins on the horse's back and returned home.

Joe Hayes looked from one to the other of the

five men who had brought him back into the saloon. Why were they being so friendly towards him? he wondered. Who cared? They were buying him another drink.

The four other members of the gang were puzzled at Finny's behaviour towards the drunk. What was going on in that devious brain of his? they wondered. There was always a reason for everything Finny did.

They sat down at one of the tables and Finny pushed Joe down by his shoulders. Matt Young fetched a fresh pack of cards from the barman and placed them in the centre of the table.

'Who else lives with you and your daughter?' Finny asked Joe.

'No one,' Joe answered.

'Good,' said Finny. 'How far away do you live?'

' 'Bout two miles on Salado Creek.'

The others frowned. What was Finny planning?

'We'll have a nice little game of poker.'

Joe shook his head. 'I've run out of money, boys.'

Finny smiled broadly at him. 'You must have something of value left?'

Joe shook his head. 'Nothing at all, fellas.'

'There's your daughter,' said Finny.

Joe frowned and looked from one to the other of them.

14

'What do you mean, boys?'

'What I mean is, you could put your daughter down as a stake. We don't play too well, so you're just as likely to win. You'll have nothing to lose and it'll be a bit of fun.'

They didn't play too well, Finny had said. It wouldn't hurt to have a game then, would it?

CHAPTER TWO

Matty lay in bed. It was dark outside and her father had not returned. She hadn't liked the look of the five men who had easily enticed him back into the saloon and she wondered why they had wanted his company so badly. The one with the guitar on his back with its strap across his chest had seemed like the leader of the gang. The look he had given her had embarrassed her with its intensity. He was not bad-looking and his hazel eyes had told her that he liked what he saw. There had not been many men who had looked at her in that way and she had to admit that it had not displeased her.

She wished her father would return, then she would allow herself to fall asleep in peace. He would usually be home by nightfall and, as the minutes and hours went by, she began to feel afraid for his safety.

Matty realized that she had fallen asleep as the sound of a horse's hoofs awakened her. She ran to the window and looked out. It was her father's horse, but there was no sign of her father.

Still in her nightdress she opened the door and looked out. The horse was waiting outside the barn where it was kept.

'Pa!' she called out. 'Pa!' But there was no reply.

Matty got dressed for riding in a pair of denim trousers and a check shirt. She picked up the lamp which was still alight, took it out to the barn and saddled up the horse she used with the wagon. She took hold of the reins of her father's horse and set off in the direction of Salado. As she rode she lifted the lamp high and pointed it in both directions along the route. A mile from town she spotted something ahead of her. When she got close she could see it was her father.

Matty dismounted and dropped the reins of both horses to the ground and ran to the prone form.

'Pa!' she yelled. 'Pa!' She shook him and then rolled him on to his back. She could see no bullet wounds in him and guessed that he had just fallen from the saddle. She was amazed that it hadn't happened before now.

Matty felt his heart then put her ear to it. She could hear it beating. She was also amazed at this.

17

After a few minutes Joe gave a groan and he opened his eyes, squinting into the light of the lamp.

Matty didn't think there were any bones broken. She tried to lift him up into a sitting position.

'Come on, help me here!' she told him sternly.

'Where am I?' he wanted to know.

'Somewhere between Salado and home. Now get up into that saddle! I've lost all patience with you.'

With a struggle Matty at last got him into the saddle. Whether or not he fell off again she didn't much care at that moment. She kept her eye on him, all the same, as they rode, and she grabbed him once or twice when he began to sway.

Somehow she got him down from the saddle when they reached home. She put her arm around his waist and half-dragged him into the house where she allowed him to fall on to his bed.

'There's something I've gotta tell you, Matty,' he began.

'Nothing that makes any sense, I reckon,' she answered, taking off his hat and boots and covering him with a blanket.

'It's pretty important,' he told her, looking up into her dark-brown eyes a little nervously.

'I reckon it can wait till morning. Now go to sleep and let me do the same!'

'Those men I was with in the saloon . . . I played poker with them but I didn't have a stake. You were my stake, Matty. They said they were no good with cards, but somehow . . . somehow they won. They won you, girl.'

Matty stopped halfway to her bed the other side of the curtain. Her heart seemed to stop beating for a second or two at what he had just said.

'And what, pray, do they intend doing with me, Pa?' she asked him.

He was silent for a few seconds before answering hesitantly:

'What men usually want with a woman.'

Matty sat down suddenly on the bed and held her hands in her lap. At last she said, 'You're not my pa. From now on I don't want anything more to do with you.'

Joe went quiet again, then said, 'You'd better leave pretty quick then, girl. They're coming for you early in the morning.'

Matty did not hesitate. She collected what few possessions she had and put them in a gunnysack.

'What will they do to you when they find me gone?' she asked him, but at that moment she felt she did not care what happened to him.

'I don't know,' he answered. 'Never mind about me. You'd best get outa here pretty damn quick.'

'Don't forget to feed the chickens in the morning,' she told him as she made for the door.

'Go up into the hills. The cabin should still be standing, I reckon,' he said.

'They're sure to get it out of you where I've gone. I'll take the rifle. I might be able to hold them off, until I run out of ammunition, anyhow.'

She picked up the lantern and stopped in the doorway.

'Goodbye, Pa. I doubt we'll be seeing each other again.'

Joe was left in darkness. A few moments later he heard hoofbeats as Matty rode away.

The morning was fresh. Mike Clancey pulled back the blanket and got to his feet. Thunder was grazing contentedly beside Salado Creek. Mike splashed some water over his face and wiped it with his neckerchief.

'Which way today, boy, eh?' he asked his horse.

After chewing on a piece of jerky and swallowing a mouthful or two of water Mike saddled up and made for a rise in the distance. From there he could survey in every direction and spot any movement.

When he reached the top of the hill he dismounted, took out the telescope from his saddle-bag and pulled it to its full extent. He swept the land below him from left to right. It was then that he spotted movement. He watched for a few minutes until the men came nearer and he was able to make out their outlines more clearly. There were six of them. One of them, he noticed, seemed to be riding with his hands behind his back. Their faces were not too clear at this point, but five of them seemed young men. The sixth, the one with his hands behind him, looked older.

The men came to a stop beside a tree. It was then that Mike saw one of them produce a rope and make a noose at one end. Mike caught his breath. They were going to hang the older man.

The man who had made the noose threw the rope over a bough of the tree which grew horizontally from the trunk, wrapped one end over it and tied it firmly. He then placed the noose over the victim's neck and wasted no time in slapping the man's horse sharply on its rump. It had all happened so quickly and Mike knew that however fast he rode towards the tree, by the time he reached it the man would be dead. Despite this knowledge, he urged Thunder down the hill and galloped towards the man swinging in the breeze.

The gang did not waste time waiting around and were soon out of sight back along the way from where they had come.

Mike reached the tree, leant across Thunder's neck and cut the man down, holding on to the rope so that he did not fall too hard on to the ground.

When he bent down to take a look at the prone figure, he heard the sound of approaching hoofbeats. Mike looked up and saw that a youth held a rifle on him.

'Hold on, boy! I didn't hang him.'

The boy came closer and took in what had happened, still pointing the rifle at Mike. When he realized that Mike had not attempted to draw his gun, he dismounted, holding the rifle above the stock near the trigger.

'Do you know this man?' Mike asked.

The youth nodded and looked down at the dead man.

'He's my pa,' came the reply, and Mike noted the catch in the boy's voice.

'I'm sorry. Do you know the men who did it?'

'I met them once,' said the youth.

'Do you know why they hanged him?' Mike asked.

The youth nodded. 'Because of me,' he answered.

The boy did not seem to want to enlarge on this and Mike did not pursue it further. He could tell the boy was in shock and it would take a while before he would be able – or wanted – to tell the whole story.

'I'll catch his horse,' Mike offered. 'I'll help you take your pa back home if you want me to?'

'They might be waiting for me there,' said the youth.

A frown flickered over Mike's brow at this. There was something strange about the boy, but he couldn't quite figure out what it was. His face was fresh and Mike judged his age to be around twelve or thirteen, yet his mannerisms made him seem older. He shook his head and turned Thunder in the direction of the hanged man's fleeing horse.

CHAPTER THREE

About fifteen minutes later Mike and Thunder caught the reins of the gelding. It looked quite an old animal and seemed glad to be brought to a temporary halt. Soon Mike was back with the boy who was sitting cross-legged on the ground staring at his father. Mike's heart went out to him. He wondered if he had any other family back home, who might ease his grief somewhat.

The boy watched in silence as Mike lifted the lifeless body of his father over the saddle so his legs and arms hung down on either side of the animal.

'Come on,' said Mike quietly. 'We'll take him back home. Is there a town nearby, and a sheriff?'

The boy nodded.

'Then I think we'd better let the law take care of things.'

Mike noticed the youngster swallow hard and he

realized that the boy did not want to speak for fear of showing his emotions.

The boy mounted his horse and Mike took the reins of the dead man's animal before mounting up himself. They set off in the direction the gang had gone.

Mike didn't want to ask the boy too many questions just yet. He would be patient and allow him to talk when he was ready.

Before they reached the house they could see a pall of smoke ahead of them and flames licking hungrily at a building.

'Not another fire!' Mike exclaimed. He hoped he wouldn't have to enter it in search of survivors as he had done in another building about a month before.

'Is there anyone at home?' Mike asked.

The boy shook his head.

'Thank the Lord for that!' said Mike in relief.

They reached the place which had been burn practically to a cinder. The boy jumped down from his horse and turned towards the chicken coop. There were dead hens lying inside.

'They didn't need to kill my chickens as well!' he wailed.

Mike realized that the boy was showing more emotion over the dead hens than he had done over his father.

'The gang were sure out for revenge! What had you and your pa done for this to happen?' Mike asked him.

The boy did not reply and had retreated back into his world of silence.

'There's nothing we can do here, son. Let's go to town. We might catch up with the men who did this.'

They rode steadily for about an hour. It was obvious that the boy's horse was no younger than his father's and speed was something they were not used to.

When they reached town Mike dismounted outside the sheriff's office and went inside. He noticed that the man inside wore a deputy's badge.

'Where's the sheriff?' Mike asked him.

'Gone after a gang who robbed the bank,' he answered.

'How many men were there?'

'Five.' The deputy frowned slightly at this tall, broad-shouldered man standing before him who looked like a saddle tramp.

'Five men hanged a man about three miles out of town,' Mike told him. 'His son's outside with the body of his pa on a horse. They burned down the kid's house and slaughtered the chickens, too.'

'Chickens, you say?'

Mike's mouth opened slightly at the deputy's

26

last words. The lawman and the boy seemed more interested in a flock of hens than anything else that had happened.

The deputy crossed to the door and went outside with Mike following.

The boy was standing beside the horses and only looked up when the deputy spoke.

'This man's Joe Hayes,' he said, looking at the corpse. 'This is no boy, mister, this here's Matty Hayes – a girl – or I should say – a young woman.'

'What!' Mike exclaimed, looking hard at the youth before him whom he had mistaken for a boy. She was trying to hide her face beneath the brim of her hat.

'What have you done with your hair?' the deputy asked her.

Matty looked at Mike before answering.

'I cut it off.'

'What did you do that for?' the lawman asked her.

'Because I didn't want the men who hanged Pa to recognize me.'

'You'd both better come inside and tell me all about it. You look as if you could use some coffee.'

Mike and Matty followed the lawman into the sheriff's office. He produced three mugs from a drawer and poured out some strong, black coffee for the three of them.

'You know my pa, Mr Watley,' Matty began.

Watley nodded. 'I most certainly do, Matty!'

'Five men came up to the saloon as I was passing with my wagon. My pa came – fell – out of the saloon. I wanted him to come home, but these men took him back inside. One of the men spoke to me and I could tell by the way he looked at me that . . . that . . . You know,' she ended.

Both men nodded. They knew quite well what the man had had on his mind.

'Pa's horse came home without him and by the time I found him and brought him back home, he told me that he'd put me up as a stake in a poker game. The men were coming for me in the morning. Pa told me to leave before they arrived. I went up to the cabin in the hills. Then . . . I thought I'd better go back home to save Pa from the men. I saw them taking Pa off and followed. I was too far away to stop them from . . . hanging him!'

Matty broke down, the first time she had shown any emotion since Mike had first met her. Both men exchanged glances and felt helpless.

'How many men did the sheriff take when he went after the gang?' Mike asked Watley.

'It was hard finding a full posse. No one seemed keen on going after that bunch. The sheriff took only three men with him. I wish there had been more.'

Mike made a quick decision. 'Deputize me, Mr Watley. I'll catch up with them. One more gun will help some.'

Matty wiped her eyes with the sleeve of her shirt.

'If you're going after them, I'm going too,' she announced.

A smile crossed Mike's lips at this.

'I'm not riding with a girl.'

'Why not? I might not be able to use a handgun and do any fancy quick draws, but I can use a rifle – maybe better than most men. I've had to make every bullet count.'

Mike gave a sigh. 'I don't care if you're the best crack shot in Texas. I'm not riding with a girl, and that's final!'

'I'm not a girl, I'm a woman. And I'm coming with you. And *that's* final!'

'What, on that horse you ride? I don't think so. I want to catch up with the posse, not catch a cold.'

Mike drank some of the coffee and turned to Watley.

'Deputize me, and I'll be off,' he told him.

'What's your name, mister?' Watley asked him.

Mike shrugged his broad shoulders and took out his pocket watch.

'I'm not sure. It could be Mike Clancey,' he said, showing him the timepiece. 'The woman in this picture could be my wife, but I'm not sure of that, either. I've lost my memory and I'm trying to find it.'

The lawman's mouth opened in surprise.

'In that case, I'll call you Mike Clancey.'

Mike got up from his chair and held up his right hand. Watley's words made him a deputy sheriff as he pinned on the star to what was left of his ragged shirt.

The new deputy was annoyed when Matty followed him to the door.

'You'd best take your pa to the undertaker, Matty,' Mike told her.

'I can't. I've got no money for a funeral,' she said.

'The county'll pay, Matty,' Watley told her.

Matty seemed relieved at this and quickly mounted up, leaving the dead body of her father still on his horse.

'Which direction did they go?' Mike asked Watley.

'North. But who can tell which way the gang would head for?'

'Before I go, have you ever heard of a place called Lodestone?' Mike asked.

Watley frowned. 'Can't say that I have. It's not around these parts, I'm sure of that.'

Mike grimaced. 'It don't seem to be around any parts.' he sighed. 'Goodbye, Matty, Mr Watley.'

He turned Thunder's head in a northerly direction. But as he started off he could hear hoofbeats behind him. He turned in the saddle.

'Go back, Matty! You're not coming with me!'

'Then where can I go? I've nowhere to live. I've got no means of support. You'll have to shoot me. Go on, shoot me!' Matty screamed.

Mike continued riding and the sound of hoofbeats followed.

CHAPTER FOUR

Mike touched Thunder's flanks with his heels to increase his speed. The hoofbeats behind him were still there, but he sensed they were getting further and further away. Mike felt mean and could only guess Matty's feelings as she tried vainly to keep up with him.

She was a determined young woman, he had to admit that. Many others would have turned their horse around and gone back.

After an hour of steady riding Mike pulled Thunder to a halt and looked back. Matty was still coming and looked small in the distance.

Mike dismounted and dropped Thunder's reins to the ground. He knew the animal would not stray. There were tracks ahead and Mike judged that there were many prints, all overlapping each other. He guessed they were those of the four possemen's horses trailing the tracks of the the five outlaws.

After a while the sound of Matty's horse became louder as it drew nearer. Mike looked at the rider, still sitting determinedly in the saddle. Then she drew up beside him.

'What kept you?' Mike grinned.

Matty liked the smiling face before her. She immediately felt safe in his presence.

'Did you bring any water with you?' Mike asked.

She looked at the pommel of her saddle and Mike guessed she had never given it a thought until he'd asked.

Mike tutted and shook his head.

'Come on, we'll follow these tracks. I hope that horse of yours can keep going. If he can't, I'm gonna have to leave you behind.'

Matty looked him squarely in the face and nodded.

'I promise I won't be a burden to you, mister. Let's get going!'

Mike remounted and rode at a slower pace so Matty could ride beside him. Out of the corner of his eye he could see that Matty kept looking at him. What were her thoughts? he wondered. He felt sorry for her but he did not want her to become dependent on him.

They followed the tracks without a stop until the light faded. She was a tough one, Mike had to admit. Not once had she complained or begged him to stop for a while.

'Do you think we're far behind them?' Matty asked as Mike pulled Thunder to a halt.

'They must be an hour or so ahead, I reckon. They'll have to stop for the night and we'll make an early start in the morning at first light.'

Matty stopped her horse and dismounted. She knew she could not have gone on for much longer.

'I'm hungry,' she told him.

'What am I supposed to do about it?' asked Mike.

'Haven't you got any food with you?'

'Have you?' he countered.

She shook her head.

'I told you not to come. If you're so darned good with a rifle, look out for a rabbit for our supper!'

'All right, I will!' she declared.

Mike found his last piece of jerky and cut it in half, handing a piece to Matty to chew on. He offered her his canteen which was almost full. He was glad he had remembered to fill it at Salado Creek.

Mike laid out his blanket roll and lay on top of it, pushing his hat over his eyes.

'I didn't notice a blanket roll on your saddle cantle,' he remarked.

There came no reply.

'You're gonna feel a mite cold tonight, I reckon.' Mike grinned.

'I'll manage. Don't you worry yourself about me, mister.'

'I'm not worrying,' Mike replied.

Half an hour passed without either speaking, then Mike sat bolt upright as the sound of rifle fire beside him made him jump. His gun appeared in his hand in a flash as he looked around him. Matty was standing a few feet away with a rifle in her hands.

'I've just got our supper,' she told him.

Mike smiled as he watched the five foot four, slimly built young woman striding away to pick up the lifeless rabbit. She obviously had good eyesight as by now it was almost dark.

She returned and flung the dead rabbit down beside him.

'You've got a knife. You can skin it,' she told him.

'OK.' Mike nodded. 'And while I'm skinning it, you can look around for something to make a fire with.'

After about an hour the two were munching on the cooked rabbit. It tasted good and, with full

35

stomachs, both felt sleepy.

Matty settled herself on the bare ground beside the dying fire. After a few moments she felt a blanket fall on her. She realized that Mike had thrown her his top blanket and he was using the under blanket to pull over him.

'Thanks,' she called out.

'Don't mention it,' came the reply.

Matty felt herself being gently kicked on her leg. Mike had been awake a few minutes before and was saddling up his horse. She pulled the blanket away and stood up.

'I'll give you five minutes,' he declared. 'Then we ride.'

While Mike saddled her horse, Matty made herself ready to ride. The rabbit meal would have to sustain them until they shot something else.

At mid-morning they saw a rider coming towards them, leading three horses. As they drew nearer they noticed that each horse carried a dead man over its saddle. Matty and Mike exchanged glances.

They rode towards the rider and, at six feet between them, Mike noticed the star on the man's lapel. This was obviously the sheriff – and the dead men must be the posse.

They stopped and regarded each other.

'I've been deputized to come and help you, Sheriff,' said Mike.

'Too late,' the lawman answered curtly. He looked at Matty. 'Don't I know you?' he asked.

'Yes,' Matty replied.

'You're . . . Matty Hayes, aren't you?'

'That's right, Sheriff. Matty Hayes minus my hair.'

Both of them could see that the sheriff was pondering on the matter, hoping for some kind of explanation.

'It's a long story.' Mike smiled slightly. 'Your deputy will fill you in when you get back to Salado. We'll carry on and find the gang.'

The sheriff looked incredulous.

'What, you two? Who are you, mister, a Texas Ranger?'

Mike shrugged his broad shoulders. 'I could be.'

'Surely you know whether you are or aren't? Even if you are, it'll take more than you and a girl to capture them.'

Matty piped up. 'I've heard that it only takes one Ranger to quell a riot. This man's got confidence, if nothing else. And I can shoot straight.'

Both men smiled at this. Mike had already seen the truthfulness of Matty's statement.

'If you want to join me, Sheriff, Matty here can take your dead deputies back to Salado.'

'Oh no Matty can't!' the girl told them force-fully. 'I'm gonna find those men who hanged my pa, even if I get killed in the process.'

Mike grimaced. 'Looks like I'm stuck with her. Have you got some more ammunition we could use?' Mike asked the sheriff. 'And mebbe some food?' he added.

Sheriff Rich Taylor found some shells in the dead men's saddle-bags and a little food.

'Not much of either, I'm afraid. The shoot-out we had took most of the ammunition. We didn't wait around in Salado to pack much food. We thought we'd catch up with them sooner than we did and then all hell broke loose. I don't think we killed any of the gang. I feel kinda guilty being the only survivor from the posse.'

'I guess they must've been waiting for you and were well hidden?' Mike surmised.

'You're right there, mister. I don't know your name?'

'Neither do I,' said Mike. 'We won't go into that now though. We'll be off. Any idea where the gang were heading for?'

'I can't say. They were heading north the whole time we were tracking them, though.'

Mike nodded. 'We'll probably pick up their trail. So long, Sheriff. I hope to see you soon. We both do,' he added, looking across at Matty.

They took their leave of each other and pretty soon, when Mike looked back, the sheriff and his dead posse were just specks in the distance.

CHAPTER FIVE

Fionbhar Carter was leaning against an overhang-
ing rock out of the glare of the sun, strumming on
his guitar as if out on a picnic with some friends
instead of having just killed four men between
them. None of the past events over the last two
days appeared to have affected him at all, but they
had. In spite of all that had happened there was
still a tiny spark of conscience inside him.

All he had really wanted was to meet up with
that girl again – the one he had spoken to briefly
outside the saloon. He could not get her face out
of his mind. He had wanted her for himself but it
had ended up that the whole gang would use her.
In a way, he was glad she had not been at her cabin
when they called for her. If he had been on his
own, he would have let it go, but the others had
different ideas. He knew he could have prevented

what happened next, but he had allowed it to happen. He knew he must be weak and it irked him somewhat.

It was Nick Bryant who had suggested they take Joe Hayes along with them and force him to tell them where his daughter was. He remembered how they had all laughed at the pathetic little man as he shakily mounted his old horse. They goaded him in turn, each one suggesting different methods of making him talk. None of them had succeeded. Not even when they came to a tree suitable for a hanging.

As Joe sat quivering in the saddle beneath the horizontal bough, Fionbhar had grudgingly admired him for not giving them his daughter's whereabouts.

They asked Joe one last time, but he remained stubbornly quiet.

Then Adam Billington whacked Joe's horse's rump with the palm of his hand and it shot off, leaving Joe Hayes dangling from the noose.

As the gang rode away, Fionbhar thought he noticed a rider approaching them, but the figure was so small that he knew he must be miles away.

The Young brothers were angry that they had not found what they had been looking for. A lighted match to some hay thrown through the cabin door would help to alleviate their ill feelings.

Slaughtering all the hens would amuse them, too.

By now the gang had been all fired up in more ways than one and they robbed the bank without any fear or difficulty. It had been too easy.

Fionbhar's long, slender fingers picked out a particularly difficult theme on his guitar. The others looked across at him and never ceased to marvel at his dexterity on the strings.

Danny Young tried to hum the tune Fionbhar was playing.

'Shut up, Danny!' the gang chorused. 'You're spoiling it.'

Fionbhar grinned at Danny's crestfallen expression.

The posse, when it arrived, was a poor turn-out. Fionbhar was quite insulted that the gang had not been seen to be worth more men in the posse. It had not taken the gang long to send them back home across their saddles instead of sitting upright in them.

Fionbhar was now quite confident that it would take quite a while for another posse to track them, if indeed, another was formed. The gang could now travel at a more leisurely pace. In any case, they would soon be over the county line.

'Hey, Finny!' Matt Young called out to Carter. 'We've got time to count out the money from the bank job now.'

'Yeah!' agreed his brother, Danny. 'Let's see how much we got.'

Fionbhar put down his guitar and walked across to his horse. He had taken charge of the bags of money personally. It would be interesting to find out what the takings were.

Carter sat down cross-legged on the ground and pulled out the bundles of banknotes first. He arranged them in piles according to denomination and handed the various piles around to the men.

'Each of you count what's in your bundle, then we'll add up the total. Then we'll do the same with the coins.'

This kept the gang occupied for quite some time. Some of them had to recount as they'd forgotten how much they'd already counted out. Tempers were beginning to get frayed.

At last the total added up to $5,000.

'I expected more than that!' Adam Billington declared in annoyance. 'It weren't worth the bother! One thousand each!' he screamed.

'It was a small bank,' Matt reminded him. 'Not too bad, considering.'

'There'll be other banks,' Finny reminded them. 'Bigger, richer banks. Be thankful you've got a thousand each. You'd have to work for more than two years in a daily job for that amount.'

Nick Bryant nodded in agreement. 'I suppose

we mustn't be greedy.' He grinned. 'We can now ride more slowly until we cross the line, and we're free.'

But the gang had not reckoned on two riders still on their trail.

Matty did not find the man riding alongside her very talkative. She still felt that he resented her presence, although he seemed as if he was prepared to put up with her company. Maybe that was because she had not given him any reason to believe that she would turn round and go back the way she had come.

As she thought more about the man, she realized that as he had lost his memory, he was unable to discuss things that had happened to him in his life, which must be the reason for his lack of conversation.

After about five miles from where they had come across Sheriff Taylor Mike picked up the trail again. Then a little later he noticed that the hoof-prints of horses led into a canyon. The hairs seemed to rise on the back of Mike's neck in warning. He had a feeling this was the place the posse had the shoot-out with the bank robbers. He looked up into the rocks but could not see any sign of movement.

The horses had obviously waited on this spot for

some time judging by the amount of dung on the ground. Mike looked further along the narrow pathway and saw that the tracks continued.

'They went this way,' Mike muttered. Matty was not sure whether he was telling her, or speaking to himself.

'Keep your eyes skinned,' he warned. 'We could be riding into a trap, although they're probably miles from here by now. They'll be heading for the county line.'

'How far away is that?' asked Matty.

'How should I know? I'm new to these parts.'

'I haven't been too far, myself,' said Matty. 'I reckon this is the furthest I've ever been from Salado in my whole life.'

Matty noticed the smile cross Mike's face at this statement. She guessed he must be thinking how boring and unexciting she must be. To Matty, riding with this man was indeed a big adventure, one that she did not want to end.

Mike dismounted and examined the tracks more closely. The horse dung had seemed quite fresh and the tracks could not have been more than an hour old. They were close. He knew they would catch up with the gang quite soon.

At noon they rested a while. Mike felt sure the gang would be doing the same and could only be a few miles away from them.

Matty sat in her preferred position, cross-legged. She took off her hat and wiped her brow with the back of her hand. It had been the first time Mike had seen her without her hat. She had cut her hair very short and it had made her look like a boy, which had been her intention, but the more Mike looked at her, the more he could see that she was a very beautiful young woman. In a way, he could understand why the gang had wanted her.

'Have you ever had a man, Matty?' Mike asked.

The question had surprised her.

'No,' she answered, frowning at him.

Mike nodded and looked away. What was he thinking? Matty wondered. Did he want to be her man?

After a few more minutes Mike said, 'Come on! We've sat here long enough.'

Matty got reluctantly to her feet and mounted up again. When would they come across the gang? she wondered to herself. Her heartbeats began to quicken at the thought. The posse had not come out of it well. Would that be their fate, too?

Two hours later Mike got out his telescope and pulled it out to its full extent. Ahead of them he could see the small figures of five men. It would not be long now before it would end – one way or the other. Mike looked across at Matty and he realized that he did not want any harm to come to her. He also realized that he would miss her when they parted company – in life, or death.

CHAPTER SIX

'Can I take a look out of that thing you put to your eye, mister?' asked Matty.

'A telescope,' Mike informed her. He handed it to her and she put it to her right eye. Mike laughed out loud when she nearly dropped it in shock.

'If I put out my hand, I could nearly touch them!' she exclaimed as a broad smile crossed her lips.

'It seems that way, don't it?' said Mike, taking the telescope from her.

'I've never seen one of them before. Where did you get it?' she asked.

'I saw it in a store window a while back. It seemed familiar to me so I must have seen one before. If only I could remember where and when.'

Matty looked pensive. She felt quite sorry for the

man riding by her side.

'If you think you remember seeing one before, maybe you'll remember other things – your name, for one thing.'

'I hope so, Matty,' he replied quietly.

After a while Mike said, 'I want to be close to them by nightfall. When they bed down for the night I want to disarm them while they're asleep. Matty, I want you to promise me you'll do exactly what I tell you. We've got to act quickly and silently. Do you understand?'

'Sure, mister.' She nodded. 'I'll do anything you say.'

'Good girl.'

They rode at a steady speed until nightfall. Mike had taken another look through his telescope and ascertained that there was about a mile between them. They would leave the horses where they were and go in on foot. He knew that the gang's horses would give them away if they knew that Thunder and Matty's horse were close by.

There was just enough light to see by as they walked quietly towards the, by now, sleeping men. At least, Mike hoped they were all asleep.

Matty dared not speak and she was sure her heartbeats could be heard in the silence.

Mike indicated for Matty to go round to the left. Mike's plan had been to creep up on the men on the ground and pick up their gunbelts. He watched as Matty made her way to the man furthest from him while he held a gun on them. She picked up the gunbelt and crept quietly towards the next one. The operation was performed until the last gunbelt was picked up. By now the belts containing guns and cartridges were heavy.

Mike realized he had been holding his breath and only exhaled when Matty came up to him, her face beaming with pride at her accomplishment.

She followed him to the horses where they had been picketed on a rope stretched between two spindly trees. Mike took the gunbelts from Matty and saw the relief on her face.

Mike threaded the rope through the horses' bridles so he could lead them all away together.

Matty was left in charge of them while Mike went back to the camp. She wished he hadn't gone. Taking the gunbelts had been too easy. Surely something would go wrong if he returned to the sleeping men? She stayed quiet and waited for his return.

A slight breeze fanned the dying embers of the campfire, giving some much needed light for Mike to see where he was going. The men had used their saddles as pillows and the saddle-bags were still attached. It was in these bags that Mike knew the money from the bank hold-up was being kept. There was no way he would be able to take them without waking the men. He wished now that he had brought Matty along with him. She would hold her rifle on them while he pulled the bags away from under their heads.

It seemed a long time to Matty as she waited with the horses. Surely he ought to be back by now?

Although he had told her to stay where she was, Matty had a woman's instinct that Mike needed her right now. She tied the horses to a tree and made her way towards Mike.

He looked up and saw her appear in the dim light from the almost dead fire. Matty was glad to see him smile at her.

Mike kicked the foot of the nearest man to him. He gave a grunt and half-woke. Mike kicked him again. This time he roused himself and half-sat up. He found himself looking down the barrel of a .45. He was about to shout out to warn the others but Mike hit him on the head with the butt of his gun. The man, Fionbhar Carter, fell asleep again.

Matty wondered why he had woken up the outlaw in the first place.

Mike decided not to wake the rest of the men before he knocked them unconscious. When he came to the fifth one, things were different. Matt Young had heard a noise and had awoken. He

51

heard Mike hit the man next to him, which was his brother, Danny.

Matt Young went for his gun and found it had gone. He stood up and faced the oncoming Mike. Matty was close by and he grabbed her arm and put her in front of him as a shield. He had a knife to her throat.

'He gets it if you shoot,' Matt told him.

Mike realized that he mistook her for a boy. He was glad that he had put the rest of the gang out of action at that moment. He hesitated for a fraction of a second before pulling the trigger of his .45. Matt Young now lay dead with a bullet in the centre of his forehead.

Matty's heart seemed to leap from her breast at what had just happened. She pulled herself away from the man's now dead hands and ran up to Mike.

'He could have slit my throat!' Matty said indignantly.

'If I'da dropped my gun, he still could've,' Mike pointed out. 'What are you griping about? You're still alive, ain't yer?'

Matty was unsure about his tone, but in the poor light, Matty noticed a smile on his face. At that moment she knew she had been safe all along.

'Now we tie their hands while they're asleep. It's much easier that way,' he said.

'Mister,' Matty began, 'I figure you are a Texas Ranger.'

'When are you gonna stop calling me "mister"?' he asked her.

'When I know your name,' came her reply.

'I've taken to using the one inscribed in the watch I've got. Mike Clancey.'

'But you're not sure, are you?' she said. 'When you know who you are, I'll call you by that name. Fer now, I'll call you "mister".'

'OK, you win!' He laughed. 'Let's tie their hands before these varmints start waking up.'

'In front of them, or behind?' Matty asked.

Mike pondered on this for a second or two.

'It's a long way back to Salado,' Mike reminded her. 'They'll need to use their hands when we stop for a break – If you get my meanin'.'

A few seconds later, Matty understood what he was saying.

'It'll be easier to bring the horses back here than carry five saddles to them. We'll need the rope they're tethered to for tying their hands. Stay here and watch them while I go and bring them,' Mike told her.

'It'd be best if you stay here and hold a gun on them while *I* go and fetch the horses,' Matty suggested.

Mike nodded. 'OK. Have it your own way. You're

probably right. If any of them came to, I bet you couldn't shoot them.'

'Huh!' was Matty's reply as she strode off to fetch the horses.

While Matty was gone, Mike pondered on what she had said. Could he possibly have been a Ranger? It was a line of thought that might help him find out who he was. He was determined now to call in at the first Ranger station he came across and ask if they knew of a place called Lodestone, or a man called Mike Clancey.

He also thought more about his riding companion. She had been of help to him in capturing the gang. Things might not have gone so well without her. She had guts, he had to give her that. She was not at all like some helpless females who relied on men for their existence. He knew she had had to be tough taking care of a drunken father. Mike wondered what would happen when they had safely delivered the gang into the sheriff's hands in Salado. Would Matty insist on riding with him from then on? What was his reaction to this question? He did not find out as Matty returned to the camp at that moment, leading a string of horses.

CHAPTER SEVEN

She was glad that she was greeted with a smile from the man wearing a deputy sheriff's badge. Was he beginning to like her a little more? she wondered.

'We'll have to get our own horses,' said Mike. 'One of us will have to mount up on one of these,' he spread his hand along the horses in Matty's charge, 'and bring ours back here. Do you want to go, or shall I?' Mike asked her.

She shrugged her slim shoulders. 'I don't mind,' she answered. 'These . . . creatures . . . aren't likely to be any trouble for a while. I'll sit and guard them while you go – if you like?' she added.

Mike nodded. 'OK. You've got your rifle, just in case. I doubt you'll have to use it, but in the last resort, don't hesitate. Understand?'

'Sure, I understand. Go on, but don't take too long, though.'

Mike picked up the dead Matt Young's saddle and put it on one of the horses. He was soon mounted up and gave Matty a wave as he left the camp.

Matty picked up her rifle, sat down cross-legged by the dead fire and waited.

Five minutes after Mike had left her she heard one of the men groan and stir. She looked across at Danny Young and watched as he gradually sat up. She could just make out his features and noticed the frown cross his face when he realized that his hands were tied in front of him. The outlaw groaned again and wondered why his head hurt so.

After a while Danny Young began to get to his feet.

'Stop right there, mister!' Matty ordered.

He did as he was ordered and looked across at Matty who was still sitting on the ground. He could just make out the features of what he thought was a boy or young man. He then looked around him and saw that his companions were still lying in their blankets and that their hands were tied also.

'Where are the others?' Danny asked her.

'What others?' she replied.

'You couldn't have done this on your own . . . could you?' he finished lamely.

'Not entirely,' Matty admitted, but did not tell

him there was only one more who was not there at the present time.

Danny noticed that his brother was not lying on his blanket roll like the rest of them, but was outstretched a little away from his bedding. He noticed also that his hands were not tied like the rest of them.

'Matt!' Danny called.

There was no reply.

Danny looked quickly at Matty. 'What's wrong with him?' he asked. 'Is he unconscious?'

'No,' replied Matty. 'He's dead.'

'No!' Danny screamed. 'You've killed my brother!'

'Now you know how it feels,' said Matty quietly.

Danny looked straight at her. 'Who are you?' he asked.

'No one of any importance to you.'

Danny looked around him again at his supine companions. He wished at least one of them would wake up.

At last, at about five minute intervals, they came round. Fionbhar Carter was first.

'My head! What happened?' The same question was asked by the others in turn.

'This kid had something to do with it,' Danny told him.

It was beginning to get lighter and Finny looked

across at Matty.

'Don't I know you?' he asked.

'We have met,' said Matty.

Finny studied her for a while longer. The face was familiar, but her clothes were not. At last, through the pain from his throbbing head, he remembered where they had first met; outside the saloon in Salado. The blood seemed to run cold in his veins. Before him was the girl whose face he had not been able to get out of his mind; the girl whose father they had hanged and whose house they had burned down.

He wanted to tell her he was sorry, but somehow the words would not come.

When the gang had all regained consciousness, Mike Clancey rode Thunder into the clearing, leading Matty's and Matt's horses.

'Good!' said Mike. 'You're all wide awake and ready to ride.'

'Who the hell are you?' Adam Billington demanded.

'I don't know,' Mike answered. 'Come on, make it quick! It'll take you a while longer to saddle your horses with your hands tied, but you'll manage it somehow.'

With much fumbling with the straps and an equal number of expletives from the outlaws, the horses were all saddled. Mike knew that all of them thought of mounting up and riding off, but he caught hold of the reins of each horse while still mounted on his own.

'What about my brother?' Danny Young asked, nodding at the body of Matt.

'Oh yeah! I'd forgotten him,' said Mike. 'Get down and put his body across his own horse. You'd better saddle it up first though. We don't want to leave some of the money behind, do we?'

Danny flashed him a vicious look but, with much difficulty, did as he was asked.

Meanwhile, Matty placed the blanket rolls on the cantles of the horses' saddles.

'Don't forget my guitar!' Fionbhar called out.

Matty picked it up and hung it across the young man's chest.

'I guess you might as well entertain us on our way back to Salado,' said Matty. 'I might even pick out a tune on it while you hang, mister.'

Their eyes met for a second or two. How Fionbhar wished they had met under different circumstances and that he had never helped kill her father.

They were off. Matty rode at the rear, her rifle within easy reach while Mike held the reins of the five horses. She wished the journey would not be so long and that they could be back in Salado within half an hour or so. A lot could happen along the way, and it worried her.

They rode until noon when Mike called a much needed halt. They all realized that it would take longer riding back to Salado than it had been riding from it as all the horses were held by one man instead of them having free rein.

Matty looked around her for some secluded place for herself for a minute or two. Mike knew of her quandary and made the gang turn away.

Matty felt their eyes on her when she returned a moment or two later.

Between them, they found a little food and refilled their canteens at one of two tributaries of Salado Creek.

As they were sitting or lying down on the ground, Mike asked, 'How much did you get from the bank?'

The gang looked at each other. It was no use not telling him as he could count it for himself and would find out when they got back to Salado.

'Five thousand dollars,' said Finny. 'A nice even sum between five of us.'

'My brother won't get his share now,' said Danny Young.

'None of you will get a share now,' Matty reminded them. 'A bit of a waste of time really, wasn't it?'

'You're not going back to Salado with the

money, are you?' Adam Billington asked. 'Surely you'll ride off with it when you've disposed of us?'

There came no reply for a moment or two.

'Was it the money you went after, mister?' Matty asked Mike.

'The reason I went after them was because of your father, Matty. Had you forgotten him? Money ain't important to me.'

Nick Bryant gave a loud laugh. 'Money's not important to him, he says! Tell us another, mister! We don't believe you.'

Mike shrugged his shoulders and a smile crossed his lips.

'Suit yourself. I don't care a damn what you think. All I know is, I'm taking you back to Salado – with all the money. Now, five more minutes and we ride again.'

There were growls of irritation from the outlaws.

Mike took out his watch and noticed the time was 12.10 p.m.

Out of the corner of his eye Mike could see that Matty was looking at him. Could she be planning to ride off with the money for herself? Inwardly Mike shook his head at this thought. But he realized that he did not know the girl that well. And $5,000 would be a lot of money for one person alone. It would set Matty up for life.

CHAPTER EIGHT

As Matty remounted, once again taking up the rear, she began to think of the future. What would she do once they arrived back in Salado? The thought of spending the rest of her life in or around the town depressed her. Although it was hard for her riding with only short stops, she knew she felt far happier than she had felt in years. Matty also knew that she had been of help to the deputy sheriff she was riding with. She began to feel pride that just the two of them had captured a band of murdering outlaws whereas the posse, except for the sheriff, had been killed. When this was all over and the outlaws were safely in the jailhouse, Matty knew she wanted to ride with the tall man who was at that moment leading the outlaws' horses.

The one they called Finny turned his head to

look back at Matty. She quite liked the look of him. It was a pity he was an outlaw, she thought to herself, but she knew she mustn't soften at all to any of them. None of them could be trusted and she must stay on her guard.

It was around four in the afternoon when Mike called a much needed halt. They would have to spend another night in the open before they reached Salado.

Matty wished they had some coffee with them. Getting back to Salado had this incentive.

Mike left Matty in charge while he walked off a little way and pulled out his telescope. He could see a band of Indians in the distance. He counted ten of them. They must have left their reservation, he guessed. Even the telescope did not tell him whether or not the braves were painted for war. With the outlaws tied, Mike knew it would be best if they could avoid the Indians. Otherwise it would only be Matty and himself to hold them off. He was not too bothered what happened to the outlaws, but over the last day or so Mike found himself concerned for her safety. His feelings for her were of admiration more than anything else.

The braves seemed to be making their way east whereas Mike and the others were heading south. As long as the Indians didn't see them, they could possibly slip by out of their way.

Mike returned to the outlaws. He knew he couldn't keep them tied for much longer and decided to let them exercise their arms for a while, but not all at once. The opportunity came for one of them when Matty asked Finny to give them a tune on his guitar.

'I need two hands for that, miss,' he replied with a grin.

Mike considered how far the sound would travel. He did not want to draw attention to themselves. On thinking it over for a second or two, he decided they were far enough away from the Indians for them to listen to the guitar safely.

Mike untied the rope around Finny's wrists. He could see that the hemp had chafed the skin. Their eyes met. Mike guessed Finny had considered whether it was worth trying to escape when his wrists were untied for a while. As the others were still tied and he did not have a weapon to hand, Finny thought better of it. Perhaps he and his friends could try something tonight? The only trouble was, they needed to speak to each other to make a plan so they could act simultaneously. This would be difficult as they were always watched by either Matty or Mike.

Finny's guitar playing seemed to relax them somewhat and all of them enjoyed the brief rest. There was not enough time to give the other outlaws a chance to be untied for a while as Mike gave the order for them to remount.

'You play very well,' Matty commented as Mike retied Finny's wrists.

'Thank you, miss.' Finny smiled down at her.

'Keep your eye on these fellas,' Mike told Matty as he strode away to take another look at the Indians. They did not appear to have heard the music and were travelling at the same pace in the same direction as before. Mike inwardly sighed with relief, although he intended keeping a watchful eye on them. He did not want them to come up behind them when his guard was down.

They rode until dusk. On a couple of occasions Matty caught Fionbhar whispering to one of the outlaws on each side of him.

'Stop that, guitar man!' Matty warned. 'I know you're plotting to escape, but you can forget it! Any more talking and I'll shoot you in the back. It won't bother me none.'

Mike turned his head to look at them and a smile crossed his face. He knew he need not worry about Matty letting him down.

They camped for the night alongside Salado Creek. It meant riding several miles out of their way as the creek took a semicircular course to their right instead of in a straight line. The fresh water was welcomed by all.

Mike decided to untie his charges one at a time so they could perform their ablutions more freely. Each was given five minutes of freedom from the ties to their wrists.

About half an hour later, when all the outlaws were once again secure, they laid out their blankets for the night. Once again they ate frugally. At that moment reaching the town of Salado seemed welcome to the outlaws, even if it was only to get a half-decent meal.

Mike knew that within the next half an hour it would be dark. He used this time to take one last look around him for any sign of the Indians seen earlier. There were none to be seen, but he would not become complacent. They could appear out of the shadows as if from nowhere. This thought suddenly hit Mike. How did he know about Indian behaviour? Had he had dealings with them before? he wondered.

'Do you want to take first watch, or second?' Mike asked Matty when he returned to the group.

'You're the boss,' she answered. 'Whatever you decide.'

'OK. You take first. I'll relieve you at around two. Don't fall asleep now!'

'Don't worry. I won't,' Matty promised him. She was pleased to receive a smile from him.

Matty found a rock and sat with her back to it.

Her rifle barrel was pointed to the ground and the stock was between her legs for easy access should she need it in hurry. From her position she was able to make out the outlines of the four outlaws and Mike, whose blanket was laid out some distance away from them.

All was quiet and Matty gave a little shiver at the thought that maybe a rattlesnake could be slithering around nearby. They had been known to get inside the bedding of anyone sleeping on the ground, for warmth. She glanced all around her but there was no sound or movement.

Mike had some premonition that something would happen that night. They were getting nearer to Salado and the outlaws were bound to make their move at any time.

Matty's eyes kept shutting but she quickly blinked them open and moved around slightly where she was sitting. She touched her rifle reassuringly to make sure it was still there, although she already knew it was.

Half an hour later Matty's head fell forward and her chin touched her chest.

One of the outlaws pulled back his blanket and stood up. He looked all around him and saw no movement from the rest of them. The girl seemed asleep as her head was tilted forward and her hands had relaxed. The rifle was resting against her leg.

The silent form hurried in a crouching position across to the girl and very gently he took the rifle. He considered shooting her but somehow he could not bring himself to do so. Instead he made his way over toward the covered form of the deputy. He had no compunction about killing him. Once he was out of the way, the gang would be free. The girl would come with them, he decided.

It was difficult to hold the rifle and pull the trigger with his hands tied, but somehow he managed it. The sound seemed very loud in the silence.

The camp was awake at once. Matty instinctively felt for her rifle and her heart seemed to drop when she realized it was not there. She stood up and looked across at where the sound had come from. A man was standing over Mike's body. He did not move or make a sound.

Matty had no fear for herself. She just had to get to Mike to make sure whether he was dead or just wounded.

'Murderer!' she screamed. She bent down beside Mike's body and pulled back the blanket. Beneath it was a saddle and a hat which fell forward. Mike's body, dead or alive, was not there.

The rest of the gang had congregated beside them.

'Matty, come here quick!'

It was Mike's voice out of the darkness. She immediately ran towards it but one of the outlaws grabbed her and held her in front of him as a shield.

Mike guessed that Matty was safe enough as only one of them had a gun. Mike took careful aim and shot the man in the heart.

'Let her go! Now!' Mike ordered.

It was Nick Bryant who held her. He knew it was useless resisting. He let go of Matty's arms and stepped to one side.

'Who did he kill?' Adam Billington asked. He walked slowly towards the outlaw who had the rifle.

Billington squatted down and looked at the dead outlaw. It was Danny Young. Now both the Young brothers were dead.

Matty came up to Mike and touched his arm.

'You knew I'd fall asleep, didn't you, mister?'

'I thought you might,' Mike answered.

'I'm sorry I let you down. I'm sure glad you didn't stay in your bedroll.'

Mike put his arm around Matty's shoulders comfortingly.

'I'm sure glad I didn't.'

Fionbhar Carter was standing nearby and his eyes met Matty's. He had planned to do what Danny Young had done a few minutes before but Danny had beaten him to it. He knew Danny wanted to get even with the deputy for killing his brother.

'The rest of you, get back in your blankets!' Mike ordered. 'We've got another ride tomorrow. You might as well get back to sleep yourself, Matty.'

'I'd rather stay awake – beside you, mister.'

Matty felt herself being drawn up on to her tiptoes to reach his lips which came down hard and firm on to hers.

Fionbhar Carter ground his teeth as he watched them before pulling the blanket over his head to shut out the sight.

CHAPTER NINE

Mike and Matty sat upright against the rock all night and Matty felt the comfort of Mike's arm around her shoulders. Both felt stiff the next morning and stretched their arms to relieve it.

'Take a walk to the creek before the others get up,' Mike advised her.

At the creek Matty unbuttoned her shirt so she could wash herself. Suddenly she was confronted by a band of Indians. Matty screamed out immediately to warn Mike.

'Indians!'

Mike hurried towards the sound of Matty's cry. He guessed they were Comanches. They sat still on their horses and looked at the two.

Mike instinctively held up his right arm with the palm of his hand out flat, facing them. How could they possibly have got to where they were in such a short time? he wondered. They were riding in a different direction when he had last seen them. Could this have been a ruse? Had they seen them and pretended they had not?

The leader or chief moved forward on his piebald horse. He stopped in the centre of the creek.

'Trade three ponies for woman,' he said, pointing at Matty.

'I didn't think they'd know the difference, you dressed like that,' Mike mumbled.

'Three ponies!' Matty exclaimed. 'I'm worth a darn sight more than that!'

'No trade,' Mike told them. 'My woman. Keeps me warm in my lodge.'

Matty looked at him open-mouthed at the lie.

The leader looked Matty up and down again, judging her worth.

'Six ponies,' he put forward.

Mike shook his head. 'I see no ponies to trade for.'

The leader looked angry. He had expected the man to be more afraid of them, that he would hand the woman over without any objection.

Mike kept calm. He knew he only had six bullets in his gun and there were ten of them. Matty had left her rifle at the camp so she would not be able to help him. He suddenly remembered the three

72

outlaws. This was the first time they had been left unattended by both him and Matty. He was certain they would take advantage of this. And they did.

Fionbhar Carter had been working hard on his bonds all night, using his teeth to pull at the knots. Just as Matty had called out and Mike had hurried to her, he had untied his bonds completely. He sprang into action and untied Adam Billington who had been lying beside him. He in turn untied Nick Bryant. Without a word they picked up their saddles, saddlebags and blankets and hurried to the horses. Their fingers still felt numb from their wrists being tied for so long and they fumbled with the straps and cinches.

Fionbhar had noticed Matty's rifle and grabbed it up.

'What about the Indians?' Adam whispered as they mounted up.

'Forget them. Let's get outa here!' Finny replied.

'But we've only got this rifle between us,' Nick reminded him. 'That deputy left our gunbelts behind when he captured us.'

'No time to waste. Come on!' urged Finny.

They set off at a canter, the sound of their horses' hoofs coming to those at the creek.

'Wah!' the Comanche leader exclaimed, raising his rifle in the air. He was expecting the men to fire at them and instinctively let off a shell at the three men. Adam Billington fell from his horse.

This distraction made Mike draw his .45. He fanned the hammer of his gun which gave him vital seconds of speed. The Comanche leader fell from his horse first and five more braves followed. Mike was now left with four others to contend with. Fionbhar Carter turned in the saddle and aimed the rifle. Mike guessed he was the target, but was surprised when three of the four remaining Comanches fell to the ground. The fourth did not waste any time and fired at Finny, then at Nick Bryant.

Matty watched as if in a trance as Mike raced towards the remaining Indian whilst the brave's attention was still focused on the last outlaw. Mike leapt up and dragged the Indian from his pony. His fist pounded repeatedly on his chin. He pulled the rifle from the Indian's hands and struck him hard on the forehead with the stock. He fell to the ground. He was only unconscious, Mike guessed. He decided to finish him off.

Matty jumped slightly at the sound of the bullet and found herself trembling.

Everything was still and quiet. It had all happened so quickly and now there were only Matty and Mike left alive.

Mike stood still and surveyed the carnage. Matty

noticed the deep frown on his good-looking features. She walked up to him and held his arm.

He did not seem to notice her at first. All this had happened before. Somewhere in the recesses of his mind he half-remembered a fight with Comanches. There were other white men there besides himself. He could hear the gunfire, the rush of horses, blood-curdling yells from the Indians, dead bodies of his white companions, a blow to his head, darkness, silence.

'Mister?'

He was brought back to the present by Matty's voice beside him.

'What's happened to you?' she asked him. He noticed the worried tone in her voice.

'All this.' He waved his arm around to indicate the dead bodies. 'I feel it happened before. I'm sure I lost my memory after such a fight as this.' Mike nodded. 'Yeah. I'm sure that's what happened. I lost my sight so I didn't see what had gone on around me. All this has made me . . . half-remember.'

He felt her squeeze his arm as if in sympathy. He looked down at her face, streaked with dust, and gently brushed some of it away.

The moment between them was lost at the sound of a low moan. It came from the prone body of Fionbhar Carter.

Both of them hurried towards the outlaw. He was on his stomach with his arms spread out. Mike pulled him over on to his back. There was a dark-red patch of blood seeping through the man's shirt close to his heart.

'I forgot my guitar,' he said quietly.

'I don't reckon you'll need it again,' said Mike.

'I'm gonna die, ain't I?' Finny asked him.

'I reckon so,' was Mike's answer.

'I'd like to play it one last time before I go.'

Matty and Mike exchanged glances.

'Go and fetch it, mister. I'll stay here with him. He won't give me no trouble.'

Mike nodded and walked back to the camp.

'Miss . . . I'm sorry we hanged your pa. I was too weak to stop them. Before I go . . . will you say you forgive me?'

Matty was sitting beside him and despite all the bad things he had done, a sudden rush of compassion came over her.

'Sure. I forgive you. My forgiveness won't stop you from heading off to hell, though.'

'Yeah. I know that's where I'm going. Miss, if you were to give me . . . just one little kiss . . . I'd go to hell gladly.'

Matty studied the young outlaw's face. His eyes were dimming and she knew he only had a few seconds of life left. Her lips came down on to his.

It was a soft, gentle kiss, and when her lips left his, she saw that his eyes were closed and she knew he had gone.

Matty looked up as she heard Mike's feet beside her. He was carrying Fionbhar's guitar.

Mike noticed the tears in her eyes.

'He's dead,' she said.

'I figured that. I'm surprised you're crying over him. I woulda thought you'd be glad.'

Matty looked away from his blue eyes.

'I don't think he was all bad. He had some good in him. He was sorry about my pa.'

Mike nodded. 'I reckon you're right. He could have killed me but he shot one of the Indians. I guess he didn't want them getting you.'

'It just leaves you and me,' said Matty. 'What about all these dead Indians?'

Mike shrugged his broad shoulders. 'The carrion will see to it. Anyhow, I don't reckon they'd want to be buried in a white man's graveyard. The horses'll have to fend for themselves.'

After a while Mike caught hold of the horses which had belonged to the last three outlaws and lifted their former owners on to their backs. He placed Finny's guitar over his head and across his back. He would make sure that the guitar would be buried with him. A slight smile crossed Mike's lips as he imagined Finny either playing to the devil, or if he had managed to get into heaven, matching tune for tune with the angels on their harps.

CHAPTER TEN

Mike handed Matty her rifle which Finny had taken from the camp.

'You'd best reload it in case you need it again,' he told her.

'All this killing,' said Matty as she surveyed the bodies.

Mike looked across at her as he led the horses.

'I don't enjoy killing,' he told her.

'I didn't say you did!' she answered a little sharply. 'You use a gun real good though. You're lightning!'

'I have been called that before. I wouldn't have lasted this long if I wasn't,' he answered as he began reloading his gun.

Matty walked beside him to the camp to pick up their horses.

'I suppose you've gone off the idea of riding day after day now?' he asked.

She shook her head. 'No, but it'll be nice to take a bath, sleep in a bed for a while and eat some proper food.'

Mike grinned. 'I can't argue with that! It won't be long now before we reach Salado,' he promised her.

Matty picked up her blanket and they continued walking to the horses. Mike was surprised that Finny and his two companions had not untied them and sent them off.

'And when we reach Salado?' Matty asked. 'What then? Do you reckon you'll get a reward for returning the money?'

'I guess so. You'll get your share of it if I do. I doubt I'd have managed without you.'

Matty looked up at him with a beaming smile on her face.

'Apart from that, what'll happen to me? When you ride off again, will you take me with you?'

She saw the frown cross his forehead at this question.

'No. For all I know, I could be married. It'd hardly be fair – to you or her – if I found I was.'

'I wouldn't mind you dumping me if you found that out. I could maybe start over in some other town. Doing what, I don't know.'

Mike shook his head. 'You'd be better off in a place you know. Something – or someone – will turn up for you.'

Matty's mouth formed a firm line and she did not speak again until some time later.

They filled their canteens from the creek and rode on, leading the five horses carrying the dead outlaws between them.

Mike was beginning to feel a certain tension between them now. He missed Matty's voice and knew that when everything was settled back in Salado he would miss her company when he rode off once again searching for his identity. It would be useless even considering taking her with him, he knew that. She would be a distraction, and a dangerous one if events forced him to use his gun once more. No, he would keep his resolve and leave her behind in Salado. She would be sure to find herself a man to take care of her.

Midday came around and the pair stopped for a break. The little food they had with them was just about gone. Mike passed Matty a slice of jerky to chew on.

'Why don't you use that telescope of yours and find us some rabbits?' Matty asked him. There was an edge to her voice and Mike guessed that he had hurt her in refusing to take her with him when he

81

left Salado. He knew he should not have kissed her, not in that passionate way. It had obviously given the girl ideas that were not intended.

Mike did as she suggested, took out the telescope and surveyed the horizon. No movement of man or animal. But then he saw them. Four men. They looked like Mexicans by their dress – leather trousers with studs down one side, big sombreros and bandoleers across their chests. Men like that were usually either cowhands or bandits. Bandits were the last thing Mike wanted to encounter. Their only objective in life was money, and the horses Mike and Matty were leading had $5,000 on board.

The riders were heading straight for them from their right and even if they rode their horses to the limit, Mike knew they would be outrun. Matty's horse was the slowest. But if she abandoned it and rode one of the outlaw's mounts, maybe they could make Salado without bing accosted? Mike broached it to her.

'I can't just leave him behind!' Matty almost wailed. 'He'll run fast, don't you worry.'

'Come on, change mounts before it's too late!' Mike implored.

She shook her head and kicked her mount in the flanks.

'Let's go!'

They rode as fast as Matty's mount would allow. But it was not fast enough for Mike's liking and pretty soon the bandits, if that was who they were, would be upon them.

'I guess it looks as if we're scared of them,' said Matty.

'And you ain't?' Mike flung back.

'I suppose I am – a bit,' Matty conceded. 'It's never dull riding with you, is it?'

Mike laughed. 'Danger sure seems to follow me around, that's for sure. You'd get tired of it after a while and wish for a nice, quiet, easy life once more.'

Matty looked to her right. 'If those greasers catch up with us, we might not have even that. It would be dead quiet.'

'They're gaining on us so we'll find out soon enough,' said Mike. 'We might as well take it easy and see what happens.'

They eased up and within five minutes the four evil-looking Mexicans drew up on either side of them. The largest of the four was unshaven like his compatriots, but was smiling, revealing uneven, tobacco-stained teeth.

'*Buenos dias, señors,*' he said in a mock-friendly voice.

Mike nodded. He noticed he had said *señors* and not *señor*. Matty had obviously fooled them into

83

thinking she was a boy – for the moment.

'You seemed to be in a great hurry,' said the one who, Mike assumed, was their leader.

'We need to get back to Salado with these.' He indicated the dead outlaws.

'I see you wear a lawman's star. Are these dead *hombres* a posse, or bandits?' he asked.

'Murderers,' Mike replied. Matty noticed that he had refrained from calling them bandits as this would mean they had stolen money and that they still had it in their possession.

'Murderers,' the leader echoed. 'How many men did they kill?'

'One in particular, and also the posse who went after them.'

The big Mexican exaggeratedly shook his head from side to side. 'I think that you are lying a little bit, *señor*. I think these men have robbed – a bank maybe?'

Mike allowed a slight smile to cross his face. 'What makes you think that, *señor*?'

'I, Miguel Ortega, know these things. I think perhaps we find out, just to make sure. Please hand me your pistol, *señor*.'

Mike nodded. 'OK, Señor Ortega. There are four of you and only two of us, so I can hardly refuse.'

The other three Mexicans went for their guns at

the same time as Mike started to go for his, but the speed of Mike's draw made their mouths open in surprise. The four bullets from his .45 flashed along the line of men before him, finding their mark in the Mexicans' black hearts. The noise startled the bandits' horses besides the string of horses Mike and Matty were leading. They had to hold on tight to their reins before they took off in alarm.

'My God!' Matty exclaimed. 'You're just one big slaughtering machine!'

Mike looked at her witheringly. 'And if I wasn't, it would be you and me lying in the dust now, Matty. Would you have preferred that?'

Matty felt as if she had been put firmly in her place and did not reply to this question.

'Do we take the greasers back to Salado?' she asked him.

He shrugged his shoulders. 'I think mebbe we've got enough without them, don't you?'

'We'll bring 'em along,' Matty decided. 'Then the folks back in Salado will know all we went through to bring back the bank money.'

Mike gave her a brief smile.

'OK. Mebbe you're right. They'll know that we've earned any reward money. I could do with a new shirt at least.'

Matty grinned. 'I agree with that, mister!'

'It's just as well we didn't bring the Indians along with us,' Mike remarked. 'If we had, there'd be more horses and dead men than live ones in Salado.'

CHAPTER ELEVEN

Mike took out his watch and saw that the time was five o'clock in the afternoon. He and Matty could see the outskirts of Salado about half a mile away. They were both heartily glad to see the place. Their experiences of the last few days had taken it out of them and both felt they could sleep for a week.

As they came to the town the people began to gather at both sides of the road to watch this strange procession that passed by. Many recognized Matty Hayes after a few seconds but no one knew who the scruffy-looking fair-haired man was who accompanied her. Behind them they were trailing nine horses with a dead body across each.

Matty and Mike dismounted outside the sheriff's office. He had heard the sudden excited babble outside and met them as they reached his door.

Rich Taylor's mouth opened wide as he looked at Salado's sudden influx of horses and their cargo.

'The stolen money is in the saddle-bags on the outlaws' horses,' Mike explained.

'What about the Mexicans?' Taylor asked him.

'I had to shoot them. They were gonna rob us.'

'You did all this?' Taylor exclaimed in amazement.

'Yeah,' Mike nodded. 'That's not counting the ten Indians. One of the gang helped me out there by shooting four of 'em before he and the last of his two friends got it. They were escaping from us at the time.'

The sheriff ushered Mike and Matty in and indicated the chairs. Meanwhile, he and his deputy Tom Watley fetched in the saddle-bags from the five outlaws' horses.

'I haven't counted it,' Mike told him. 'The gang said they'd stolen five thousand dollars.'

'That's about right,' Taylor nodded. He straight away opened up the first bag and counted out one thousand dollars. His deputy assisted him and counted out the rest.

'Yes, with the coins, it makes five thousand.' Taylor looked hard at Mike's face.

'You're a complete stranger, mister, yet you brought back the money. You could have ridden off with it all, never to be seen again.'

Mike nodded. 'True. But the thought never occurred to me.'

'You're a rare one and no mistake,' said Taylor.

'He should get some reward for his honesty, I say,' Matty put forward.

'Oh he'll get a reward, I'll see to that! We'll go over to the bank right away,' the sheriff enthused.

'Before we do, how about a cup of coffee?' Mike asked him. 'Matty and me could sure use one.'

Watley and Taylor laughed out loud at this.

'I just bet you could!' Taylor said. 'Tom, get the mugs out. We'll all have one.'

'I sure needed that!' Matty exclaimed when she had finished the long-awaited drink.

Mike nodded in agreement.

'You know, Sheriff,' Matty began as they walked to the door, 'this man only went after the outlaws because they hanged my pa. The money they stole was incidental. He only killed three of 'em because they used me as a shield when they tried to escape. The Indians killed the others.'

Both lawmen looked at each other, then at Mike and shook their heads in astonishment.

'You'd better get these dead men to the undertaker,' Mike suggested. 'The horses want seeing to as well. I'll take mine and Matty's to the stables before we go to the bank. Feeding them is more important than the money.'

Matty suppressed a grin at Mike's words as she could tell he was becoming more of an enigma to the lawmen by the minute.

'And this man,' Mike indicated the body of Fionbhar Carter, 'he should receive special treatment. He shot four of the Indians as he was making his escape. If it weren't for him, Matty and me wouldn't be here now. He wanted to be buried with his guitar, so make sure that happens.'

'Tom, will you see to that while I take this man to the stables?'

'Sure thing, Rich,' the deputy replied.

'I can't keep calling you "this man". You told me you didn't know your real name, so what shall I call you?'

'I go by the name on this watch.' Mike took it out and showed it to him. 'Matty will only call me "mister",' he grinned.

Rich Taylor had already tipped out some papers that were in a box and put the $5,000 inside, so his hands were full. He was glad when Mike and Matty's horses were put in the charge of the stable owner and they could take the valuable box to the bank.

' 'Evening, Sheriff?' the teller greeted the lawman.

' 'Evening, Claud. Get Mr Downey out here, will you?'

'Right away, Sheriff.' He returned a moment or two later with the bank manager.

'I'd like to bring this through, Mr Downey,' said the sheriff, indicating with his eyes the quite heavy box he was carrying.

The dour-faced banker guessed the box contained something of importance or value, and ushered Taylor through to the back. Matty and Mike followed.

'This man—' Taylor began.

'And this woman,' Matty interjected.

'And this woman,' Taylor added, 'went after the men who robbed this bank. They've brought back every cent of it. They deserve some recompense for the considerable trouble they've been through to get it, don't you think?'

The dour face of the banker brightened up somewhat.

'Of course!' he exclaimed. 'When you came back with the dead posse, Taylor, I gave up on the idea of getting the money back. What would you say to ten per cent between you?' he asked, looking from Mike to Matty.

Matty looked up at Mike for an answer.

Mike shrugged his shoulders. 'Fine by me.'

'How much would that be – each?' Matty asked.

'Two hundred and fifty dollars – each,' Downey answered.

91

'Why! that's more money than I've seen in my whole life!' Matty exclaimed. 'I can pay for my pa's burial and have lots over.' It was obvious that her father had only just come into her mind. 'Has my pa been buried yet, Sheriff?'

'Not yet, Matty. We weren't sure if you'd be back, but I suggested Bob Miller, the undertaker, hold on for a week. Now you're back, he can go ahead with the burial.'

Matty nodded and looked downcast.

'Now that Bob's got all those bodies you've just brought in, Mike, he's going to be a busy man.'

'Sorry about that, Sheriff,' Mike answered with a trace of a smile on his lips.

Meanwhile Downey had unlocked the safe and taken out some banknotes. He counted out two piles of $250.

'There we are. And thank you for your honesty, young man.'

'If the sheriff had had better luck, he would have done the same.'

'Yes, but that was my job,' Taylor reminded him.

'I was deputized, so it was my job.'

Taylor grinned and nodded.

The bank manager shook hands with Mike and Matty and the pair left the bank with Taylor.

'I'll call in at the undertaker's first,' said Matty, 'then we'd better book ourselves a couple of rooms. *And* a bath!'

'Is there a store in town that sells clothes?' Mike asked. 'It'd be no use putting the rags I'm wearing back on after a bath.'

'Sure, over there at the Webbs's general store.' Taylor pointed.

Mike accompanied Matty to the undertaker and arranged for her father to be buried the next day, then booked two rooms at the hotel.

'How long for?' the clerk asked them.

Mike looked down at Matty. 'I can't say right now. About a week. That should give me a chance to rest up before moving on.'

'And you, miss?' he asked.

'The same, I reckon,' she answered. Mike noticed that she did not look him in the eyes. 'And we both want a bath laid on. While you're seeing to it, we'll do some shopping.'

Half an hour later they left the general store carrying parcels wrapped in brown paper and made their way back to the hotel.

'When you've bathed, I'll meet you for supper in the hotel dining-room,' Mike told her.

'Oh yes! *Food*! *And lots of it*!'

CHAPTER TWELVE

Mike was first to arrive in the dining room. It was seven o'clock. Little did he know the trouble Matty was going to to look her best before she sat down in front of him at the table. He looked up when she eventually arrived and he found himself giving an involuntary gasp at her transformation. She had on a plain yellow dress with white lace around the neck. Her hair had been washed and although short, was still becoming as it surrounded her face in loose waves.

She sat down and gave him a big smile.

'Matty,' he said hesitantly, 'you look . . . beautiful!'

She lowered her eyes shyly then looked him straight in his blue ones.

'You look pretty good yourself, Mike.'

He laughed. 'So at last you're calling me Mike

instead of mister.'

'I think it's about time I did.'

The waiter came over.

'What have you got that's tasty and filling?' Mike asked him.

'Steak,' he offered.

'Anything else?' Matty asked.

He shook his head. 'Most folks seem only to ask for steak.'

'Maybe that's because they know it's all you've got?' Matty suggested.

'Possibly,' the waiter answered glumly.

'OK. Steak it is – for two. With all the trimmings,' Mike told him.

As he went away Mike took Matty's small hands in his large ones. 'I can't get over how lovely you are. Some lucky young man will snap you up in no time.'

'What if I don't want to be snapped up?' she asked, her previous expression changing into a frown.

He let it pass.

'Will you come with me when they bury my pa?' she asked.

'Sure.' He nodded.

After their meal they sat for a while talking. Matty filled Mike in on her life so far, and as she spoke she realized just how empty it had been, scraping a living and barely existing on the little money she made. She began to feel worried about the future. Her share of the reward, $250, seemed a lot of money to her, but she also knew that it would not last that long, especially as she could not support herself and had no home. If only Mike would ask her to go with him when he left Salado.

They climbed the stairs to their rooms and stopped outside.

'You can . . . come in for a while . . . if you want?' she suggested.

He looked down at her in the dim light in the passage. He wanted to, desperately, but he knew what would happen if he did. He couldn't let anything happen between them as soon he would be leaving her in Salado.

'I don't think that's such a good idea, Matty,' he said as he took her hands in his.

'OK. We'll get an early night then. See you at breakfast.'

Her upturned face forced him to kiss her, long and firmly on her lips.

'Sure,' he said to her last words. 'Make it eight.'

She nodded. 'Goodnight, Mike.'

Her coquettish smile remained with him after she had closed the door.

*

Having no clock or pocket watch in her room, Matty had no idea of the time when she awoke the next morning. She had expected to fall asleep almost at once, but could not get the man in the next room out of her mind. She knew he had wanted her the night before, yet he had refused her subtle offer. She tutted to herself as she stepped out of bed. What did that make her? It was obvious that he was far more of a gentleman than she was a lady. She began to wish she had not asked him into her room. Matty remembered the two kisses he had given her; one while they were with the outlaws and the other the night before. Somehow, they had turned her from a girl into a woman – and she liked it.

She asked the man on the reception desk what the time was and was informed it was 8.30. Her heart jumped slightly. She was late.

The dining-room had two other guests, both at separate tables. Mike was not there.

She waited. She refused breakfast when the waiter approached her.

'We'll order when Mr Clancey comes down,' she told him.

Still she waited. What had happened to him? she wondered worriedly. Had he left town without saying goodbye? Inwardly she shook her head. No, he wouldn't do that, surely?

At last Matty got up from the table and went into the lobby.

'Have you seen Mr Clancey this morning?' she asked the desk clerk.

'No, miss,' he replied.

She nodded and decided she would knock on his door.

There was no answer. She tried the knob. It was locked from inside. She knocked again – louder.

After a minute or so she heard movement from inside the room.

'Mike! Are you OK?' she called.

The door was unlocked from inside and it opened a fraction. Mike stood there, wearing his trousers but minus his socks, boots and shirt. Matty felt her heart flutter at the sight of his bare, broad chest.

'Sorry,' he said. 'What time is it?'

'You're the one with the watch,' she answered. 'You look at it enough times.'

'I couldn't sleep last night. I was sure I would drop off at once.' He grinned. 'I blame it on you.'

She returned his smile a little shyly.

'Give me a few minutes, will you?'

'Sure,' she answered. 'We've got all day – except for a few minutes while they bury my pa.'

Mike had entirely forgotten this appointment at the graveyard. He noticed that Matty was wearing a grey dress and bonnet this morning.

She walked back down the stairs and waited in the lobby for him. Within five minutes he was by her side. It felt good when he took her arm and led her into the dining-room.

The day before, Matty had arranged with the undertaker to meet at the graveyard at ten o'clock. The grave had already been dug. There was no preacher present and Matty informed Mike that Salado had no church and no one of any denomination to perform any services. The undertaker read out a few words from the Bible when the pine coffin had been lowered into the ground.

'Goodbye, Pa,' Matty said quietly. 'I hope where you're going there'll be plenty of whiskey.'

They watched as the earth was thrown into the hole until a mound appeared on the ground.

Mike put his arm around Matty's shoulders comfortingly and they left the quiet scene.

They were met on their way back by the sheriff, Rich Taylor.

'We've just buried Pa,' Matty informed him.

The lawman nodded. 'I'm sorry, Matty. I'm glad I've met you. I want to let you know the town's giving you and Mike a dance and feast in your honour. It's to be held in Rob Miller's barn from five o'clock till midnight.'

Mike frowned. 'Why?' he asked.

'Why?' Taylor repeated. 'Because you both deserve some recognition for what you did.'

'We've already had a reward,' Mike reminded him.

'This is extra,' Taylor told him. 'Come along and enjoy yourselves. Everyone's eager to meet you and shake your hand, Mike.'

'They can shake my hand, too, if they like,' Matty added with a cheeky grin.

Taylor laughed. 'Yes, I'm sure they'll want to do that, Matty. You'll be danced off your feet by all the men in town, so I should get a good rest before tomorrow. By the way,' he added, 'no guns to be worn, Mike.' He had noticed that Mike was not wearing one at that moment in recognition of the solemn occasion earlier.

'Mm,' Mike mumbled. 'I don't feel dressed without my gun. But I guess it'll be easier for dancing. I don't even know if I can dance. I can't ever remember doing so. Mebbe it'll come back to me. I pity any woman's toes if she dances with me, though.'

Matty looked up into his eyes. She hoped he would not ask too many other women to be his partner.

CHAPTER THIRTEEN

Mike felt uneasy at the prospect of attending a gathering in his honour. The longer he stayed in Salado, the harder it would be to leave. He knew he was becoming too fond of the beautiful young woman by his side and the sooner he left, the better it would be for all concerned.

'I'm gonna get a few provisions from the store, Matty,' he told her.

As she looked up into his blue eyes she knew at once what his intentions were. Her heart sank but she tried hard not to let it show. Instead she smiled up at him.

'OK. I'm going over to the bank to open up an account. I don't feel too safe with all that sudden money coming into my possession.'

Mike nodded. 'See you in a few minutes.'

There were four people waiting to be attended

to ahead of her. She was in no hurry and looked around the place. She had never been inside a bank before yesterday, never having had any spare cash to withdraw or deposit. It gave her a wonderful feeling of independence.

It was now her turn and she handed over one hundred dollars.

'I'd like to open an account with this money,' she told the teller.

'A good idea, miss,' he replied. 'If you leave it in long enough, you'll get interest on it.'

Having her back to the door, Matty did not notice the four men who entered, each pulling on a mask over his face.

'Get over there by the wall and keep your hands where I can see them!' one of the men barked.

Matty's heart gave an involuntary jump at the suddenness of it. She was the last to respond to the order.

The bank teller had his hands in the air and Matty noticed that they shook slightly with fear.

One of the would-be robbers lifted up the counter opening and went behind it.

'Open up the safe and make it quick!' he growled.

The bank manager appeared and his mouth opened wide in astonishment.

'Come on, open it up!' the same robber told

him, pushing the manager in front of him towards the back of the bank.

Another of the men hurried forward to help stuff the money into a gunnysack he had with him for the purpose.

Matty had become used to dealing with criminals over the last few days and she decided to remain calm. Maybe Mike would come over to see her and sort it all out. But maybe he would get shot as the robbers left. Her heart began to beat a little faster at this awful thought.

The few customers remained quiet with their hands in the air. Only one man had a gun which was quickly taken from him in case he became emboldened and used it.

At last the two men came out of the door behind the counter, the sack one of them was carrying was bulging.

'Let's git!' said the first heading for the exit.

The one at the rear surveyed the four would-be customers. Matty caught his eye but she could not see the smile cross the robber's face beneath the mask. He made a grab for her and pulled her in front of him as a shield.

'No one follows – or she gets it,' he declared. 'Tell that to any posse!'

Matty was propelled out of the door and thrown on to one of the waiting horses. The rider quickly jumped up behind her and the four masked men together with the one who'd been minding the horses charged out of town. As no shot had been fired, no one had taken much notice until they saw the masks covering the outlaws' faces.

At any moment Matty expected a gunshot from behind her but guessed the bank customers had warned everyone not to fire in case she got hit.

A moment or two later Mike Clancey came out of the emporium carrying several packages. One of the bank tellers ran up to him and Mike could see by the man's face that something was amiss. The teller obviously remembered Mike from the day before when he and Matty received their reward for returning the money from the previous robbery.

'The bank's been robbed again,' he told Mike. 'They took Matty Hayes hostage. They said that if anyone followed them, they'd kill her.'

Mike's blood seemed to freeze in his veins at the anxious man's words. The thought of anything bad happening to Matty made him realize just how much she had come to mean to him.

Having just come from burying Matty's father Mike remembered he was not wearing his gun which was back at the hotel. Thunder was also not to hand and would have to be collected from the livery stable.

'Get the sheriff!' Mike told the teller. 'Tell him to meet me here and be ready to ride.'

'But the robbers said they'd kill Matty if anyone followed them,' the teller reminded him.

'I reckon she's safe for now. Now go on, and hurry!'

The teller nodded and ran down the street towards the sheriff's office.

Mike raced up the stairs to his room at the hotel and buckled on his gunbelt. He picked up his parcels from the bed where he'd put them, then charged back down the stairs. He reached the stables in double quick time and saddled Thunder himself. He distributed his parcels into both saddle-bags. The contents would come in handy during their search for Matty and the outlaws.

Within ten minutes he was back in the main street where Rich Taylor was waiting for him.

'We haven't had a bank robbery in years, then you show up and we get two,' said Taylor.

The slightest glint of a smile crossed Mike's face at this.

'Come on, let's ride!' was Mike's reply.

'Won't we need more men?' asked Taylor.

'No. The fewer the better. We'll try and catch up with them before nightfall. They'll have to stop then.'

'I guess you're right. It only took you and Matty

to bring back the other outlaws. I don't know how you did it, but I'm sure you know best,' said Taylor.

Mike gave the sheriff a thankful look. He knew the man could so easily demand that he took charge of the situation himself, being a lawman, and it was a great relief that Taylor had such faith in him.

They wasted no more time and were riding in the same direction that Mike and Matty had gone before. The outlaws had about half an hour's start on them and Mike knew they would be continually looking over their shoulders to see whether they were being followed. Mike felt sure that they would be expecting any posse to be far larger than just two men, and they would be less likely to feel threatened.

After a while Mike sensed that they were being followed. He took out his telescope and opened it up.

'Ah,' said Rich Taylor. 'So that was your secret weapon!'

Mike grinned. 'Everyone should have one, Sheriff.'

As Mike put the telescope to his right eye, Taylor could see by his companion's expression that he had seen something in the distance.

'Someone's following us,' said Mike. 'He's about twenty minutes or so behind.'

'Friend or foe?' Taylor asked.

'That's for us to find out. But not yet. We've gotta get closer to the outlaws – and before nightfall. I reckon Matty will be safe until then.'

Rich Taylor looked Mike Clancey in the eye. He knew what the man was thinking. Matty didn't stand a chance of holding off one man, let alone five.

'See those rocks up there?' Mike pointed forward. Rich nodded. 'Make for them and we'll wait for that feller to catch us up. I don't like being sandwiched between two factions. We'll find out who he is and what his intentions are.'

'Do we hurry?' Rich asked him.

'Not too much. I don't want him to know we know he's following us.'

'Right,' Rich answered.

They made it to the rocks and dismounted. Both drew their .45s and waited.

It didn't take long before the rider reached them.

'Drop your weapon and dismount!' Mike ordered.

The man was taken by surprise. He was tall and wore a dark moustache to match the hair showing beneath his hat. He looked around forty. He hesitated a fraction before complying with Mike's request.

Rich Taylor picked up the man's gun from the ground.

'What's your business?' Mike asked him.

'Same as you. I'm after the bank robbers. I've been trailing them for nearly a month,' he told him.

'You a bounty hunter?' was Mike's next question.

'No. I'm a Ranger.'

Mike's ears pricked up at this last reply. He remembered the feeling he had had during the skirmish with the Comanches while he was with Matty. He half-remembered it happening before and the word 'Ranger' seemed to ring a bell.

'Do you know a man named Mike Clancey?' Mike asked.

Taylor shot him a surprised look. This was the name Mike used.

'Maybe,' the newcomer replied.

'Do you, or don't you?' Mike snapped.

'Is he a friend of yours?' the man asked.

'That's what I want to know,' said Mike. 'Do you know who I am?'

The man looked at him for a long half-minute.

'Maybe.'

'I'm gettin' pretty tired of that word, mister. Do you know me?' Mike demanded.

'What's your name?' he asked.

Mike shook his head. It was obvious that this man did not know him. For a second or two Mike felt deflated.

'Do you know a place called Lodestone?' was Mike's next question.

'Sure.'

Mike's heart seemed to skip a beat.

'How do you know it?' Mike asked him.

'There was a battle there. It's a mining town and the Comanches surrounded it. A man named Mike Clancey took command and saved the town. He was a Ranger – so I heard anyhow,' the man added.

'Were you there at the time?' Mike asked him.

The man shook his head. 'No. I heard all about it though.'

Mike let out a deep sigh. He was no nearer finding out whether he was Mike Clancey or whether he had obtained the watch he carried from the real man. At least this man before him might be able to help him find the town of Lodestone and he could then find out his true identity at last. But before that there was the problem of the fleeing outlaws to sort out. And Matty's safe return.

CHAPTER FOURTEEN

The ride was, for Matty, an uncomfortable one, having to share a saddle with the outlaw. She was angry more than anything. She had just obtained $250 as a reward for bringing back the hold-up money from the previous bank robbery and had handed back $100 for safe keeping in an account. She vowed she would never trust a bank again.

Despite her predicament, she had an inner smile. She was not likely to receive any more money to put in a bank ever again. In fact, she doubted if she would live to see another day.

The men rode their horses hard, putting miles between them and any posse that might follow. Matty knew they were hoping that no one would follow, having her as a guarantee against it.

They rode until well after noon, then all seemed

to have decided together that a break was needed.

Matty was dragged from the horse and she stumbled slightly. Up until now they had all kept their neckerchiefs over their faces.

'Ten minutes, then we ride again,' said one of them who, Matty guessed, was their leader. He pulled off his mask and his and Matty's eyes met. The others pulled off their masks also.

'Now she's seen our faces, we'll have to kill her,' another of the gang pointed out.

The leader allowed a brief smile to cross his craggy face.

'I guess so,' he drawled. 'But not before we find out what she's got under them petticoats of hers.'

The others laughed and seemed to take a step towards her.

'I must say you're mighty brave – I don't think so!' Matty flung at them.

'You don't need to be brave to get what you want in life, missy,' said the leader. He took a step towards her. 'Now don't you struggle none. It'll go much easier on you if you don't fight.'

Matty's insides seemed to turn a somersault. No. This couldn't be happening. Her eyes looked wild as they were cast over the men approaching her.

Rich Taylor pointed towards the hills about a mile ahead.

'That's where the other outlaws picked us off. I kinda feel ashamed that they didn't get me as well.'

'There's no need for that, Rich,' Mike answered. 'It just weren't your time to die. You were needed for this ride.'

Rich Taylor gave Mike a small smile in appreciation.

'At least we'll be more ready this time. If they're up in them hills, they'll have the advantage over us,' said Mike. 'If we take a detour around and come out the other end, ahead of them, we might stand a better chance?'

The Ranger and Taylor gave a slow nod as they thought about it.

'It might just work.' Taylor nodded.

They veered right, away from the hills.

'They might not be up there, waiting for us,' the Ranger pointed out.

'It's best to be safe than sorry,' said Mike.

'I'd rather know for sure,' said the Ranger. 'They might not be up there, and we might find ourselves still behind them,' he added.

'If we get close, we'll know it soon enough. They'll want to pick us off as soon as they can to get us out of the way once and for all.'

If they had carried on along the trail that Rich Taylor had taken once before, they would have had to go through a pass, with rocks on either side. It was now noon and they were out on the open plains with the hills behind them.

'I'm going back aways to see if there are any tracks,' Mike informed his two companions. They nodded and dismounted, intending to take a short rest until he returned.

Mike approached the pass, his sharp eyes roving around him. There were indeed tracks of five horses. Mike knew they had passed that way some time before and that he, the Ranger and Taylor were behind them. He looked up at the hills and did not see any movement.

Mike knew the outlaws would have to stop at some point and he feared for Matty at their hands.

Matty gritted her teeth and tried hard to stop her heart from beating out of her chest.

'Now hold on a minute!' she ordered. 'Answer me one question.'

The outlaws exchanged glances and all had frowns on their faces.

'What question might that be, missy?' the leader asked.

'What would you rather have – twenty-five thousand dollars . . .' she hesitated, '. . . or me?'

They laughed, guessing she was just playing for time.

'Wal,' the leader began, 'I'd sure like to have

both. Where's this twenty-five thousand dollars you're talkin' about?'

Matty placed her right hand on her hip and looked them full in their eyes.

'You don't suppose I'm gonna tell you,' she scoffed. 'But I will if you leave me alone. I give you my word. And I always keep my word.'

The leader grinned broadly. 'OK. We give you our word that we won't touch you – until after we get our hands on this money you're on about.'

Matty shook her head. 'That's not good enough. You get the money and you keep your dirty hands off me when you get it. If you don't keep your part of the bargain, I have ways and means of making you wish you had. I'm no feeble female. I got that money from a bank job and hid it. I've been living the life of an ordinary woman since, but I've had my secret stash to visit now and then so I can live comfortably without being suspected.'

'Lady, I don't believe a word of it,' the leader told her. 'Are you tellin' us that your purity is worth twenty-five thousand dollars?'

'Mister,' she began, ' "my purity" as you put it, is worth a darn sight more to me than that. What's it to be?' she asked levelly.

'Tell us where the money's stashed and two of us'll fetch it while we leave you here with the others.'

Matty looked the leader straight in the eye again and did not blink.

'No deal, mister. We all go together. You won't find it without me. No one could find it without me. I hid it very carefully.'

'Let's take her now, Ned,' another of the outlaws said. 'We'll get it out of her where the money's hidden afterwards. She'll give in after we've finished with her and beg for mercy.'

Matty now knew the leader's name was Ned. If she was patient, she might learn the names of the rest of the gang.

'Which direction do we go to find this money?' Ned asked her.

'We've already passed it. We'll have to go back.'

Ned shook his head slowly. 'You're stallin', girl. You're expectin' a posse to come after us and you want us to run into them. That's your plan, ain't it?'

Matty shook her head. 'There's one man back in Salado who'd stop any posse forming. He cares about me more than a little so he wouldn't want to cause my death by following.'

'It won't be just you the posse'll come for. They might find the hold-up money's more important. If we go back the way we came, we'll ride straight into them. If they're in that pass, they'll have an advantage over us,' Ned pointed out.

'True,' Matty nodded. 'But won't twenty-five thousand dollars be worth the gamble?'

The men were quiet for a few minutes while they pondered over the matter.

'Tell me this,' Ned began. 'How did you get hold of twenty-five thousand dollars from a bank hold-up?'

Matty gave an enigmatic smile.

'Because I took part in the raid,' she replied. 'Oh, I wasn't dressed like this!' she exclaimed, indicating her dress. 'No one knew who I was as I dressed like a man and I wore a mask. I was able to return to Salado and change back into a woman.'

'What happened to the rest of the gang?' another of the outlaws asked. 'It must've bin a mighty big haul to share it between you.'

Matty shook her head. 'No. Only twenty-five thousand dollars.'

Ned frowned deeply and looked down into her dark eyes.

'What happened to the rest of the gang?' was his next question.

'What do you think?' she replied.

CHAPTER FIFTEEN

Rich Taylor and the Ranger looked up expectantly at Mike's return.

'Any sign?' the Ranger asked.

'Yeah. It looked like the tracks of five horses,' said Mike.

'I reckon they'll have had to take a break by now,' Rich commented. He looked at Mike and knew what he was thinking. Rich was thirty-seven and had never married. He wondered what would happen after all this ended. What were Mike Clancey's real feelings for Matty Hayes? She was a fine-looking young woman and if Mike left the picture he knew he wouldn't mind courting her himself.

'Let's ride,' said the Ranger. 'The sooner we catch up with them devils, the better.'

Mike nodded and his two companions

remounted. They set off once again.

'Have you got a name, mister?' Rich asked the Ranger.

Both Rich and Mike noticed the extra long hesitation before he answered.

'Sure,' he said. 'Which one do you want?'

Rich gave a short laugh. 'Don't say we've got two here who don't know who they are?'

The Ranger frowned and looked at Clancey.

'My full name's Ezekiel Jeremiah Obadiah Micah Powell. Beat that!' He grinned.

Both Mike and Rich laughed.

'Nope. Neither of us can beat all those names,' said Mike. 'Which one do you use?'

'Zeke,' the Ranger replied. 'Come on, names ain't important. Let's ride!'

The three touched their horses' flanks with their heels and soon covered the next two miles.

Mike dismounted.

'They stopped here,' he said. He led Thunder as he inspected the ground in all directions. His two companions noticed the deep frown on his face.

'It looks as if they're heading back the way they came!' he exclaimed.

'But we would have seen them,' said Rich.

'Not necessarily.' Mike shook his head. 'They went off that way.' He pointed to his left. 'They'll use those rocks for cover, then my guess is, they'll end up behind us.'

Zeke pursed his lips. 'I don't get it. Why would they do that – unless they aim to pick us off so we don't follow them.'

'Yeah, that's their plan.' Rich nodded.

'Mebbe,' Mike muttered.

'You don't think so, Mike?' Rich asked him.

'We haven't set eyes on them so far,' said Mike. 'I don't reckon they've seen us, either. I've a feeling they've got another reason for coming back. I only wish I knew what it was.'

The outlaw called Ned had Matty on the front of his horse. He was enjoying the feel of her close against him but Matty was not.

'You'd better not be lying to us,' he said in her ear. 'If you are . . .' the rest of his sentence hung in the air.

'You're gonna kill me whether I'm lying or not,' said Matty. 'You might as well find out one way or another.'

Ned growled. He had the feeling this girl in front of him was playing them for fools and he did not like it.

As they rode Matty tried to look all around her. She had not spotted a posse and began to wonder if she ever would. If Mike was heading it she knew he would make sure they were not spotted and would somehow creep up on them. Night would be the most likely time. While she had ridden with him in search of the gang who had killed her father, she had come to know his methods. She was sure he would catch up with this gang also, and release her. She kept this thought with her for comfort as they continued their ride towards the pass.

As the Ranger, Mike and Rich rode in the direction in which the tracks indicated that the gang were going, Rich Taylor began to have doubts about Zeke, the Ranger. If he really was a Ranger. So far he had let Mike do all the tracking and make all the decisions. What if he was an outlaw himself and was only after the hold-up money? He knew he and Mike were unlikely to find out – until they met up with the outlaws. And then . . . Rich gave an involuntary shiver. They would be sandwiched between Zeke and the gang. Rich knew he and Mike would have to find out somehow before they met up with them. He would have liked to get Mike on his own for a few minutes and put his fears to him, but it seemed unlikely he would get an opportunity. He only hoped that Mike might get suspicious about the Ranger also.

Darkness seemed to fall quickly and Matty realized

that they would not reach the pass before it was completely dark. She hoped the men would keep their promise not to touch her, but she had the feeling they might not keep it. The last time she had caught up with outlaws she had had her rifle and also Mike Clancey to keep her safe. Now she had neither.

Mike was riding behind Zeke with Rich following on behind.

'How long have you been a Ranger?' Mike asked the man.

Both he and Rich noticed the hesitation before Zeke answered. It seemed that Zeke always hesitated instead of replying immediately, as if considering his answer very carefully.

'Nigh on five years, I reckon,' came the reply at last.

'This town of Lodestone I asked you about before. Which direction is it from here?'

Again Zeke hesitated. 'I guess it's west. Along the Rio Grande.'

'Darn it!' Mike growled. 'I've been riding for months looking for the place and I've ridden in the wrong direction.'

'What's the fascination with Lodestone, anyhow?' Zeke asked him.

'I could have been there once,' Mike replied.

' "Could have?" I reckon you'd remember if you had,' said Zeke, slowing down a little to let Mike draw up beside him.

Mike shook his head. 'That's the problem. I can't remember. I don't even know whether my name's Mike Clancey or not.'

Zeke shook his head and frowned.

'I've got a watch here.' Mike took it from his vest pocket and handed it to the Ranger. The man took it. 'I don't know if it's *my* watch or whether I got it from the real Mike Clancey. I took the name as I don't remember what my name really is.'

'Wal, I'll be . . .' Zeke exclaimed. 'I can see why you want to go to Lodestone to find out for sure. Can't you remember how you lost your memory?'

Mike shook his head. 'I got a crack on the side of the head, but I don't know how. I could be an outlaw or a lawman. I do know that I'm pretty good with a gun which has come in useful a time or two. Some folks have even called me Lightning.'

'I guess we'll find out when we meet up with the outlaws we're following,' said Zeke. 'If you are an outlaw, you'll ride off with all the money.'

Rich was by now beside the two of them. 'We could say the same about you, Ranger – if that's what you really are.'

Mike and Rich did not miss the dark look which crossed the other's face.

'I told you I'm a Ranger, and that's what I am,' he answered angrily.

Mike exchanged looks with Rich, but let it pass. He took out his telescope and opened it up. The other two waited until Mike had surveyed the land ahead of them and to both sides. He passed the telescope to Rich and pointed in a southerly direction, the direction from which they had come.

'Yeah!' Rich exclaimed. 'I can just make out specks moving in the distance.'

'Let me see!' Zeke asked, holding out his hand to receive it.

They waited until Zeke had spotted the movement some miles ahead of them.

'I don't reckon we'll catch up with them before nightfall,' was his comment.

Mike gave a deep sigh. 'I reckon you're right.' Dusk was already falling.

CHAPTER SIXTEEN

Rich Taylor noticed a different expression come to Mike's face. Obviously some other thought had just crossed his mind.

'I'm damned if we're gonna just sit here and wait until morning before we catch up with them. Come on, let's ride!'

The other two men exchanged glances.

'OK. It's fine by me,' said Rich. Zeke did not say anything but mounted his horse.

'The nearer we get to them before nightfall, the better it'll be. I just hope Matty will be safe . . . but I'm not countin' on it,' Mike said.

The three started off at a canter and did not speak again until in the fading light they could barely see a few feet ahead of them.

'You ain't thinking of riding all night, are you?' Zeke asked.

Mike shook his head. 'It wouldn't be wise. But at least we'll be nearer to them than we would have been.'

'True,' said Zeke. 'I don't know about you two, but my insides are growling for something to eat.'

Mike dismounted and opened one of his saddlebags.

'Here, some cheese and jerky,' he said, throwing two packages to Zeke. 'I bought it at the store before we left as I intended making an early start the next morning. Then the bank was attacked, so it's lucky I was ready. The last time I rode after outlaws I didn't take any food with me.'

'What did you do?' Zeke asked.

A grin crossed Mike's face as he remembered.

'Matty shot a rabbit. It was the best goddam rabbit I've ever tasted.'

'This Matty sounds quite a girl,' said Zeke.

It was Rich who answered.

'She sure is! I'd be mighty honoured if she was my woman.' He gave a quick look at Mike to see if he had already staked his claim on her, but Mike just gave an enigmatic smile.

The three men tucked into Mike's food and then turned in for the night.

When Mike and Rich woke at first light they noticed that Zeke was not where he had been lying the night before. And his horse was gone.

The two men exchanged glances.

'I didn't trust that man from the very start,' said Rich, and Mike noticed the anger in his companion's voice.

'Has he gone ahead to get all the glory, or has he gone to warn them?' Mike voiced his thoughts.

'Whichever, we'd better be on our guard from now on,' was Taylor's opinion.

The two were soon mounted up and heading in the direction they had last seen the outlaws travelling. The only sign of Zeke was his horse's hoofprints.

When it grew lighter Mike put his telescope to his eye and looked around. A single rider was ahead some two miles away. Mike was unable to see any signs of the outlaws.

Matty had tried to get as comfortable as possible on the hard ground that night. Ned had thrown her a blanket but this had not helped her much. She dare not sleep for an hour or two, fearing one of the men would try and molest her, but Ned had warned them not to break their bargain with her. Twenty-five thousand dollars was far more important than a few moments with the girl. There would be plenty more women to have after they got their hands on the money. She eventually drifted off and awoke the next morning to the sound of voices.

As her eyes became accustomed to the early morning light she noticed that all the men were standing, facing the same direction, and each had a gun in his hand.

'It's me, Ned, Zeke,' the man called out before riding into the camp.

'You sure took your time!' Ned answered. 'Where did you get to and what took you so long?'

'After I fixed my horse's shoe I figured you'd gone into the next town. Your tracks led that way, anyhow.' Zeke grinned broadly. 'I found out that you decided to pull a bank job there, too. You took a girl hostage, I heard, so no one would follow you. Two did. One of them was a sheriff. I left them back on the trail aways during the night and rode until I caught up with you now.'

Matty's heart seemed to skip a beat at his words. He had said that one of them *was* a sheriff. Had he killed Mike and Rich?

Zeke looked around him and his eyes focused on Matty.

'This must be the hostage,' he said, nodding towards her.

'Yeah. It's lucky we picked her for a hostage. Seems she robbed the same bank as us and has the money stashed away somewhere in that pass a way back.'

'What's your name, girl?' Zeke asked her.

She told him.

'Matty, eh? Seems like I heard of that name only yesterday. You a friend of a man called Mike Clancey?'

Matty did not answer at once. Mike had probably let it slip that she had helped him bring in the other bank robbers.

'No. Never heard of him,' she replied, hoping he would believe her.

'She's lying,' Zeke told them. 'This Mike Clancey, or whatever his real name is, said that a woman called Matty rode with him and helped him bring in some bank robbers. He said nothing about them robbing a bank.'

'Wal, he wouldn't, would he? He was pretending to be on the side of the law.' Ned frowned. 'She seemed to be tellin' the truth.'

'Women *never* tell the truth. I shoulda thought you'd known that by now,' Zeke said angrily.

'We were riding back to the pass to make sure,' said Ned. 'It seems a shame to pass up an opportunity to get our hands on twenty-five thousand dollars.'

Zeke looked hard at Matty and sighed.

'What did you do with this fella Mike Clancey, and the other one – the sheriff? You killed them both I hope?' Ned asked.

Matty's blood seemed to freeze in her veins at Ned's words.

'Of course I did. Shot them while they slept. We won't be getting any trouble from them.' He laughed evilly, and looked at Matty. He could see the stunned expression on her face at what he had just told them.

'What are we gonna do?' one of the gang asked. The thought of riding away without finding the money did not appeal to him. On the other hand, they could all be wasting their time.

'There's no money in that pass. You can bet your last dollar on it. Get me some coffee, then we get outa here. And not back to the pass either.'

Ned's lips were pressed into a firm line. He had been in charge while Zeke had seen to his horse's shoe, and he had enjoyed making all the decisions. Now Zeke was back, his power was being taken away from him.

'I say let's put it to the vote,' Ned suggested. 'All those of you who want to go back to the pass raise your right hand.'

The men looked at each other before deciding. Whether the money existed or not, the mere thought of getting their hands on it was enough to sway their decision. Matty watched in fascination as each one in turn raised their right hand.

'You're out-voted,' Ned told Zeke. 'Get some

coffee goin', someone – then we ride – to the pass.'

Mike and Rich were riding also. In the same direction.

CHAPTER SEVENTEEN

Matty was beginning to get worried. Soon they would find out that she had been lying to them and she shuddered at the thought of her fate. Mike and Rich could not save her now. Tears came into her eyes but she quickly blinked them away. She was determined not to let the gang know how she felt.

Rich noticed that Mike made no attempt at conversation as they rode together. He could tell by his companion's expression that he was a worried man.

At last Mike said, 'I don't get it. If Zeke's one of the outlaws, why didn't he kill us while we slept last night?'

Rich shook his head. 'It don't add up, does it?'

'I'll reserve judgement on the man until we meet up again. It could be that he got in with the gang to gain their confidence, to make it easier to bring them in. I'm wonderin' if his motives are more than just going after the loot. Maybe they killed his partner. I'm not sure.' Mike frowned as he thought about it. 'Do Rangers ride in pairs, groups, or alone?'

'I can't say I've had much to do with them,' Rich answered. 'Could be any of those. I still say we can't trust him.'

Mike nodded and shrugged his shoulders. 'I guess we'll soon find out one way or another.'

Zeke drank some coffee one of the men handed him. He nodded in acknowlegement.

'How much did we get from the Salado bank?' he asked Ned.

'*We?*' said Ned. 'I don't seem to remember you being with us when we robbed it. Why should you get a cut?'

'Because,' Zeke began, 'my horse lost a shoe. Besides, I got rid of your tracks before a posse arrived on the scene. They went off in the wrong direction,' Zeke lied. 'If I hadn't been left behind, they would've caught up with us. I did my part in preventing it, so I deserve a cut. How much did *we* get?'

'About fifteen thousand,' another of the gang told him. He knew, as he had counted it himself.

'With the twenty-five thousand we'll get at the pass, I reckon we can retire very comfortably,' was Ned's opinion.

Zeke smiled slightly and shook his head.

'I can't see that happening somehow,' he said. 'You lot will drink and gamble it all away in a matter of months – weeks even. If you don't get shot or hanged before that.'

'Pessimistic critter, ain't he?' Ned laughed. 'I'll take my chances, Zeke, and so will the rest of us. Now let's get outa here. At least we have no fear of them two lawmen catching up with us.' Ned laughed out loud. 'We're free now and can take our time.'

Zeke did not answer this but his eyes rested on Matty.

'The woman rides with me!' he declared.

'Don't I get a drink first?' Matty asked. 'If I pass out you won't know where I hid the loot.'

A slight smile crossed Zeke's lips and he indicated with a nod of his head that she should be given a mug of coffee.

'We can't have you passin' out on us now, can we?'

Their eyes met as Matty took a long drink from the mug. Her throat was dry and she felt slightly

133

revived as she handed back the mug.

The men quickly cleared the camp and mounted up. Zeke lifted Matty up on to his horse and got up behind her. He let the others go in front of them and Matty felt he was dragging behind slightly. She frowned. Just what was in this man's mind? she wondered.

'Now listen, lady. Don't speak, just listen,' he told her in little more than a whisper.

'I'm not an outlaw, I'm a Texas Ranger. I've been instructed to infiltrate the gang and become one of them. I'm gonna bring them in when the time's right. If I'da been a real outlaw I'da shot that Mike Clancey and the sheriff back there, but I didn't. Don't let on to the others what I've just told you. I know there's no money somewhere in the pass we're headin' for. What was the idea telling them that?'

Matty turned her head slightly and spoke in the same whispered tone.

'They were gonna . . . you know . . .' she began.

'Sure, I get it,' came his reply in her ear.

'I told them if they'd leave me alone I'd show them where I'd hidden the proceeds of a bank robbery I took part in.'

Zeke suppressed a laugh at this.

'You must've been convincing to make them believe that!' he said.

'Now I suppose you'll tell them,' said Matty.

'No. We've both got a secret to keep,' he whis-pered in her ear. 'By keeping it, we'll both stay alive.'

Matty was still not entirely sure she believed the man behind her, but somehow she felt he might come in useful against the rest of the men. She dreaded reaching the pass, as then they'd find out the truth.

'I don't think this is gonna work,' said Mike. 'We've gotta go around them and be in front, not behind. We've gotta take them by surprise. They're expecting us to be on their tail.'

'If we only knew exactly where they're heading for it would help,' Rich replied.

'I've still got the feeling they're heading for that pass. Mebbe Matty's told them something to make them believe going back to the pass will be to their advantage. But what?'

Rich gave it some thought before replying.

'If we turn back now, we'll reach the pass before they do. We can hole up somewhere and wait for them. On the other hand, if they're not heading for the pass, we'll have let them get away.'

'Decisions, decisions,' said Mike. 'Something's tellin' me we go back to the pass. You can shoot me if I'm wrong.'

Both men laughed, although uneasily. It helped break the tension and worry they were both feeling.

Matty noticed one of the gang turn in the saddle and look at her and Zeke. By the expression on his face she could tell he felt uneasy at Zeke's being behind him.

'I guess you're the Matty that Mike Clancey spoke about,' said Zeke quietly when the outlaw in front turned back in the saddle.

'What did he say?' Matty asked him.

'He was mighty impressed with you,' said Zeke. 'He said you were good with a rifle and killed your supper when you were riding after a gang of outlaws.'

'He's pretty good with a gun himself,' Matty told him. 'He's like lightning. In fact, Lightning has been his other name. He's not a man to come up against, that's for sure.' She hesitated for a few seconds before adding, 'I guess I shouldn't have told you that. You might not be telling me the truth that you're a Ranger and not an outlaw.'

'It's the truth,' he assured her. 'How was it that you and he were going after a gang?' he asked.

'They hung my pa, then robbed the Salado bank. A posse had already gone after them, but they were ambushed in the pass we're heading for.

Only Rich Taylor, the sheriff, survived. I followed Mike – he didn't want me to,' she added. 'We met up with the sheriff on his way back to Salado with the dead posse on their horses. Mike and I continued and, well, we got them and brought them back. We had a bit of trouble with some Indians and they killed one or two of the gang who were escaping at the time. On our way back to Salado some Mexican bandits wanted the hold-up money we were taking back to Salado. Thanks to Mike, they didn't get it.'

'Wow!' Zeke exclaimed. 'And you really were taking the money back? You didn't hide some of it for later?' he asked.

'We returned it all,' Matty assured him. 'Mike and I were given a reward. I was just opening an account at the bank with some of it when they' – she indicated the men in front of them – 'held up the bank and I was taken hostage.'

'Your life ain't exactly been uneventful, has it?' He laughed quietly.

Matty shrugged her shoulders. 'I reckon not. Not lately, anyhow. I wouldn't mind a little peace and quiet for a change.'

She felt Zeke's arm come more securely around her waist. Somehow she knew it was only an act of reassurance on his part and nothing more. She had to admit it gave her some comfort. She also had to admit she would need more than this in the hours to come and knew that there would be much bloodshed. She just hoped none of it would be hers.

CHAPTER EIGHTEEN

Mike and Rich rode hard back the way they had come. Their intention was to ride through the pass, hide up in the rocks and wait for the gang.

When they reached their destination Mike rode out further, leaving Rich to find a place to leave the horses out of sight. Mike took out his telescope and surveyed the landscape in front of him. He made out the gang far in the distance and was gratified to see they were coming his way.

'They'll be here in about half an hour, I reckon,' Mike told his companion when he returned to him.

'I've found an inlet in the rocks which'll hide the horses,' said Rich.

'Good. We'll have the advantage over them above their heads. But they'll have the advantage over us with Matty as a hostage. I surely hope that we can get her out of this safely.'

Rich nodded. He was just as worried about Matty as Mike was.

A little over half an hour later the gang arrived at the pass. They all looked above them in case a posse was waiting for them, but were not too concerned. Zeke had said that he had killed the two-man posse, so it was unlikely that anyone would be waiting for them.

Mike and Rich backed out of sight at the arrival of the men. They had noticed that Matty was on the front of Zeke's horse. Both men frowned. Was this a good thing, or bad? If only they knew who Zeke Powell really was; a Ranger or an outlaw?

Zeke spotted the two men up in the rocks but the rest of the gang had not.

'Matty, get down and hide yourself somewhere beyond the mouth of the pass,' Zeke told her, and helped her down. She did as she was told without question.

'Hey, what's goin' on?' Ned demanded when he turned in the saddle and noticed what had happened. 'Get that woman back here!' he yelled.

Ned saw that Zeke's gun was now in his hand, pointing directly at him.

'Throw down your weapons, you men. You're surrounded.'

Zeke knew that this was not entirely true as only

Mike and Rich were above them, but it made the men stop and think for a fraction of a second.

Ned had no intention of dropping his gun. He drew and fired it at the same time as Zeke fired his own. Mike and Rich saw that Zeke had killed the man he had fired at but Zeke himself had taken a bullet in his left arm. He was holding the wound with his right hand.

At least now the two posse men knew whose side Zeke was on. They were now free to open fire.

'Do as the man said and drop your weapons!' Mike shouted down at the men. 'Do it now – or you're all dead men.'

The gang looked up in a panic, their horses turning in circles in the small space. They were not expecting this at all. They all went for their guns and Mike and Rich could see that they had no intention of dropping them, but of using them.

As the gang aimed up at the rocks, each fell from his saddle, dead. Zeke had replaced his own .45 and sat still in the saddle, holding his arm as he waited for Mike and Rich to climb down to him.

Rich felt numb at what had just occurred. The last time he had been in this same pass he and his men had come under fire from above them. He marvelled at how his life had been saved, which he guessed must have been through some divine intervention.

Mike shook Zeke's hand and both men grinned at each other.

'Thanks for saving Matty,' Mike told him.

'My pleasure,' said Zeke. 'Someone had better go and find her.'

'I'll go,' Rich said eagerly and nudged his horse's flanks with his heels. He found Matty hiding behind a rock about twenty feet from the mouth of the pass. Her eyes were wide and frightened, but quickly changed to pleasure at seeing Rich.

'Is Mike OK, and Zeke?' she asked.

'Mike's OK, but Zeke took a bullet in his arm. I guess he could do with some doctoring.' Rich smiled. 'Are you OK, Matty? Did any of them . . . hurt you at all?'

She shook her head and came up to him and put her arms around him. Rich's heartbeats seemed to quicken at the closeness of her and he could feel her sobbing into his chest. At last she looked up into his grey eyes.

Rich lifted her on to the front of his horse and they rode back to the pass.

Matty saw the dead bodies of the outlaws and she began to tremble at the shock of all that had happened to her. She had hardly gotten over chasing after the first gang of outlaws before she had been dragged off by another gang.

'I could say that I want to go home,' Matty whispered. 'But I haven't got a home to go back to.'

'You'll always have a home with me, Matty,' Rich told her.

She looked from one man to the other. She hardly knew Zeke, but he had turned out to be her saviour. She knew Mike Clancey a little more, and had believed that she was in love with him, but somehow she knew deep down that he would never stay with her in Salado, nor would he ask her to ride with him. She looked again at Rich Taylor. She had known him for years, but not well. What was he exactly offering her? she wondered. What would go with a home?

'Tell me something, Matty?' Mike began. 'What are you and the gang doing back here?'

She had now been brought back to the present from her thoughts.

'I had to make up some story to stop them from . . . you know?'

The men nodded understandingly.

'I told them if they'd leave me alone, I'd show them where I'd hidden some money from a hold-up job.'

'What hold-up job?' Rich Taylor frowned. 'You and Mike brought the other bank raid money back to Salado. The whole lot of it.'

'They didn't know that,' she smiled slightly.

143

'They believed me, anyway.'

She looked at Mike. 'How did you know we were coming back this way?' she asked him.

Mike pulled out his telescope. 'Remember this?' he grinned.

She laughed. 'Yes, I well remember that. Your magic eye.'

Matty turned to Zeke. 'Let me take a look at that arm,' she said, pulling his hand away from the bloodstained shirt.

'You'd better sit down,' Mike told him. 'You look as if you might fall down if you don't.'

Zeke did as he was told and knew that he had done it none too soon. He was beginning to feel faint.

'Mike, tear off his sleeve for me,' Matty told him.

Mike produced a knife from the sheath on his belt and sliced easily at the material. He inspected it.

'I reckon the bullet's still in there, Zeke. We'd better get it out. Anyone got any whiskey?' Mike asked.

'Now's not the time to be drinking whiskey?' Matty admonished.

'I didn't intend for any of us to drink it, Matty!' Mike smiled at her slightly. 'I need it for disinfecting the knife.'

Matty's mouth opened in an 'Oh' as realization

dawned on her.

'I know some of the gang have got some whiskey in their saddle-bags. They were always taking swigs at the bottles.'

Rich and Mike hurried towards the horses that were waiting to carry their owners once more. They inspected each saddlebag and besides a couple of bottles of whiskey, they found bundles of money from the bank hold-up. They took it also.

Mike handed the money to Rich Taylor and began pouring some of the whiskey over his knife.

'This is gonna hurt, Zeke,' Mike warned him. 'Don't be afraid to cry out if it helps,' he added.

Zeke felt in no condition to pretend to be brave and waited for the first probe of the knife.

Matty was sitting on the ground with Zeke's head on her lap, stroking the man's forehead and face soothingly. She felt him flinch at the pain and held his shoulders firmly.

After a couple of probings, Mike pulled out the bullet with the point of his knife, then poured some more whiskey into the wound.

'We need some bandages,' said Mike. He looked at Rich Taylor.

'It's no use asking him,' said Matty. 'You and he don't wear petticoats.' With that, she pulled up her dress and proceeded to tear strips off her petticoat and handed them to Mike.

Between them, Mike and Matty bandaged Zeke's wound as best they could as a temporary measure until they got him back to Salado to receive more professional help from a doctor.

'Best let him lie there a while,' said Mike. 'While he rests, you might like to count out the money we found in the saddle-bags,' he said to Rich.

'The gang stole fifteen thousand dollars?' Matty told them. 'So they said, anyway.'

'They should have more than that, added to the money we took from a bank before Salado,' Zeke told them a little weakly.

Mike looked down at the man and thought how pale he looked.

'Did you take part in it, Zeke?' Mike asked.

'Yeah,' Zeke confessed. 'I was ordered to infiltrate the gang and then bring them in.'

'So anything over fifteen thousand dollars belongs to another bank?' Rich queried.

Zeke nodded, then passed out.

'Let him sleep,' Mike suggested. 'It'll do him more good.'

While Zeke slept, Mike and Rich counted out the money and put it in two piles; one pile of fifteen thousand dollars and the other of twenty thousand.

'No wonder the gang said they could retire on the proceeds of both bank jobs together with the expected amount they thought I'd hidden.' Matty smiled.

After they had finished counting out the money Mike knew this was the end of his task. He handed out to his companions some of the food he had bought from the Salado store, which was for his journey to find the town of Lodestone. Zeke was still sleeping.

When Zeke awoke at last Mike told him of the division of the money and put Zeke's hold-up money in the man's saddle-bags. Mike handed him a mug of coffee which Zeke drank thankfully.

'Are you fit enough to ride yet, Zeke?' Rich asked him.

'Sure. I've gotta get back to my station.'

Matty shook her head. 'Not yet awhile, you're not!' she said emphatically. 'You're coming back with us to Salado to get looked at by a doctor.'

Zeke smiled. 'OK. But I'll leave as soon as he has looked at me.'

Zeke was helped on to his horse and Matty sat behind him to make sure he did not fall from the saddle. Rich mounted up and noticed that Mike hesitated before mounting Thunder.

'I'll say goodbye now,' said Mike. His eyes roved over the horses, each with a dead man across the saddle. How often it seemed that he had seen this sight before. How many more times would he see it? he wondered.

'You're not leaving us?' Matty exclaimed. 'You can't leave us!'

'Sorry, Matty, but I must go. I'm sure you'll be taken good care of . . . by somebody.' His blue eyes twinkled as he looked at Rich Taylor.

'It was nice knowing you, Rich. And you, too, Zeke.'

'Will you ever return?' Matty asked him.

Mike noticed the catch in her voice. He hesitated and looked for the last time at her beautiful face. He would have liked to have said "yes", but he couldn't.

'I doubt it. Take care, Matty. I'll never forget you.'

And with that, they watched as he rode through the pass to head in a westerly direction to follow the Rio Grande.

CHAPTER NINETEEN

Mike Clancey rode steadily on, passing San Ambrosia Creek, El Indio, Eagle Pass, Quemado, Pinto Creek, and Del Rio. He stopped occasionally to top up supplies for his journey from a town or village. There were times when he remembered that he had passed through some of the places before. If only he had known which way to go from the start it would have saved so much time. A wry smile crossed his lips as he thought about it. If he hadn't gone the wrong way he would never have met the people who had become part of his life for a while.

His journey took a little over a month until he came to Del Rio and here he learned that the next habitation was a place called Lodestone. Mike's heart seemed to jump when he at last found someone who knew where the place he had been searching for was.

He set off again and had a strange sensation within him. After all this time he was sure he would at last find out his true identity.

Mike rode in early in the morning; the town was only just awakening. He stopped outside the general store just as the door was being unlocked. The storekeeper nodded in acknowledgement as Mike dismounted outside. Then a frown crossed the small man's face.

'Don't I know you, mister?' he asked.

Mike smiled eagerly. 'Do you? I hope so. Do you know my name?'

The storekeeper gave Mike one more look before replying, 'I surely do! Why, you're that Mike Clancey, the Ranger, who helped the town out of a sticky situation.'

Mike grinned, relieved.

'And what is my name, mister?' Mike asked.

The man gave a little laugh. 'Don't you know your own name?'

Mike shook his head. 'I somehow forgot it along the trail. Remind me.'

'Unless your his double, you're Mike Clancey.'

Mike took the man by his shoulders and smiled down at him.

'Thanks, mister. You've made me a happy man!'

He hesitated a while before he asked, 'Do you

know where I come from? I've kinda forgotten that, too.'

The storekeeper shook his head in disbelief.

'What happened to you? Did you get a crack on the head or something?'

Mike nodded. 'That's exactly what happened. I've spent the last six months trying to find out who I am.' He took out the familiar watch and showed it to the man.

'Although this watch is inscribed Mike Clancey, I wasn't sure whether it was mine or not. Who could tell me where I'm from?'

'I suggest you call in at the next Ranger station, seeing you're a Ranger. I reckon they'll have been wondering where the hell you've got to.'

Mike nodded. 'I bet they have! Where can I find them?'

'Back a way' – he pointed east – 'in Del Rio.'

'Del Rio!' Mike exclaimed. 'I've already called in there. I asked them where Lodestone was, not where there was a Ranger station. I didn't even remember I was a Ranger.'

Mike started to remount Thunder but the store-keeper called him back.

'Come on in for a mug of coffee and some breakfast before you go, Mr Clancey. It would be an honour to have you here in my establishment.'

Mike had felt a rumble in his stomach just

before that and agreed. He felt sure he would offend the man if he refused.

Late afternoon found Mike back in the town of Del Rio. He looked around him and finally found a place with the words RANGER STATION in bold lettering on the building. Mike made for it and dismounted outside.

Three steps led him on to the boardwalk and he entered the door.

Inside a large man was pointing at a big map of Texas on the wall and explaining to a tall, thin man that this was the place he wanted him to go to.

Both men looked round on Mike's entrance and both men's mouths dropped open in surprise.

'Well I'll be . . .' the larger of the two exclaimed. 'If it ain't Mike Clancey! Where the hell have you been all this time? Did you run out on your partners and leave them to be killed?'

Mike removed his hat and twisted it around in his large hands. Before he had a chance to answer the thinner man said, 'As your body weren't with the others, we thought you'd either ridden off or were captured and tortured by them damn Comanches.'

'Well, he sure as hell don't look tortured to me,' said the big man. 'They wouldn't have let him go alive, either.'

152

'Sorry, but I can't say what happened to me. Only that I must have got struck on the head and when I came to I couldn't see a damned thing. I whistled and Thunder came up to me so I got on somehow and he took me to a town. After a while my sight returned but to this day I can't remember a thing of what happened to me. I've been searching all down the Rio Grande but no one could tell me where Lodestone was. This watch,' Mike produced it yet again, 'had Mike CLancey engraved in it and Lodestone. I met up with a man who said he was a Ranger and he told me the direction where Lodestone was. When I reached there a man recognized me and directed me here.'

Both men looked at each other and then back at Mike.

'Wal, if that don't beat all!' the larger man exclaimed. 'Is that the truth?' he asked searchingly.

'It sure is,' Mike replied. He stepped forward and showed the two men his watch. 'Can you tell me who this woman is?' he asked. 'Am I married to her?'

Again the other two looked at each other in bewilderment.

'Sure. That's your wife,' said the man who seemed in charge.

'Her name's Frances. You call her Fran,' said the other.

'Where can I find her?' Mike asked them. He felt in need of a sit down and pulled up a chair.

'About three miles outa town,' the big man began. 'She grows vegetables, keeps chickens and does some dressmaking to make ends meet. She comes into town once a week and sells produce to the store and women come to her for her dressmaking skills.'

Mike put his elbows on his knees and covered his face with his hands. He felt a hand on his left shoulder and Mike looked up into the big man's face.

'What do I call you both?' Mike asked them.

The big man answered. 'I'm George Merryweather – Captain,' he added. 'And this is Tom Galloway. We're short-handed after the Comanche massacre. Will you be resuming your post here?'

'I can't answer that just yet,' Mike told them. 'I've got to get home first. Has . . . Fran found another man while I've been gone?' he asked hesitantly.

'Not as far as I know, she hasn't,' said Merryweather. 'You'd best get off home and get reacquainted with your wife, then, when you've sorted yourself out, call back and see me if you want your old job back.'

Mike stood up and nodded. 'Thanks. One more

thing, where do I live?'

Merryweather ushered him to the door and pointed left down the street.

'Follow the track out of town and after about an hour's ride, turn left at the copse of trees and follow the track for fifteen to twenty minutes. You'll see a house in front of some hills.'

Mike shook Merryweather's hand and remounted Thunder.

'Thanks, Captain.'

They exchanged smiles and Mike rode off down the street.

'What do you make of that, Cap?' Galloway asked his superior.

The big man shook his head slowly. 'I guess it'll take a while for him to sort his life out again. We'll just have to wait and see if he'll rejoin the Rangers.'

CHAPTER TWENTY

Mike rode steadily towards the place where Merryweather told him he lived. As he got nearer he got a strange feeling in his gut. He had met trouble and danger over the past six months but had never felt like this. It was as if he was afraid.

What kind of greeting would Fran give him? Would she be glad to see him or had she become accustomed to his absence?

The copse of trees was where Merryweather said it would be. Here he turned left and carried on towards his home. Would he recognize it once he saw it? he wondered. Would he recognize his wife? He felt his stomach churning in apprehension.

Then he saw it. His house built of logs with a hill behind it. In the distance he could see a woman hoeing between vegetables of some kind. A man was near the barn with a pail in his hand. Who was he? Had his wife taken another man in his place?

He saw that she looked up and ran to the house, picking up a small child from the stoop before entering. She came out a moment later carrying a rifle which she put to her shoulder.

Mike rode on towards her. As he got nearer the woman seemed to relax her hold on the rifle and held it by the stock. She began to walk slowly towards him and as recognition dawned on her, a smile came to her good-looking features.

'Mike!' The word came out almost inaudibly. She ran to him.

Mike dismounted and looked down at her face with the dark hair surrounding it – just like in the picture he had looked at in his watch so many times.

'I believe I'm your husband,' Mike told her.

A frown crossed her face.

'Are you playing games with me, Mike? Of course you're my husband! Where have you been all these months?'

Yes, she looked like the picture he carried with him. But did he remember her? He had to admit that he did not.

'George Merryweather told me your name was Frances – Fran. Is that right?' he asked.

'Mike, stop it! Answer me! Where have you

been, and why are you acting so strangely?'

The man Mike had seen near the barn had now come up to them. Mike did not recognize him but a feeling of jealousy came over him. Who was this man and what was he to Fran?

'Hello, Mike. Where the devil have you been all this time. We thought you were dead?'

'Who are you, mister?' Mike asked him.

The man gave a short laugh. 'You know darn well who I am. I'm Fran's brother. I've been helping her while you've been gone.' He waited a moment or two before continuing. 'You know my name's Dan – Dan Benson. What's come over you?'

'For the past six months I've been travelling around Texas trying to find out who I am and where I came from. Fran . . . I don't remember you – or you, Dan. My memory might return at some time, but it's like I've just met you for the first time. You'll have to be patient with me. I've got a lot of catching up to do.'

Mike looked towards the house.

'Fran, did I see you with a child?' he asked.

She nodded. 'Don't you remember our son either?' she asked with a catch in her voice.

He shook his head. 'No. I've got a son.' A broad smile crossed Mike's face. 'I've got a son,' he repeated.

Dan took Thunder's reins and led him to the barn and allowed Mike and Fran to become reacquainted.

Mike looked around the neat room with three doors leading off it. He was home at last.

A little boy was sitting in the middle of the room and looked up at the tall man who had just entered. Mike picked him up in his arms and examined him closely.

'How old is he, Fran?' Mike asked.

'Two years old tomorrow.'

'I've come back just in time for his birthday. What's his name?'

'Michael – after you.'

'Michael,' Mike repeated. He felt well pleased. He put the boy down on the rug again and took Fran in his arms and held her close to him. It felt good. It felt good to Fran also.